THE BLOCKED TRAIL

Because he turned aside from the trail a moment to look into a pair of dazzling, feminine eyes, Dan Riley, Ranger, allowed wanted men to escape.

How he took the trail after four outlaws, to either capture or slay them and vindicate himself, how he met them, one by one, how those same feminine eyes aided him and righted the wrong they had done, is told in "THE BLOCKED TRAIL" —a trail blocked by intrigue, by violence, by gunplay, hard riding and hard fighting, but over which Dan Riley traveled, hurdling all obstacles.

Some men called him "Romance" Riley in derision. Then he became known as El Sombrero, because on the leather band of his hat the names of the four were carved, to be burned off one by one as he got his men.

And then he found real romance when he least expected it, and won his heart's desire after he had accomplished his mission and could look his superior officers in their faces again.

"THE BLOCKED TRAIL" is a dramatic chunk of life in the raw, swift in action, rich in humorous moments.

THE BLOCKED TRAIL

by

JOHNSTON McCULLEY
AUTHOR OF "THE FLAMING STALLION" AND "A WHITE
MAN'S CHANCE," ETC.

WILDSIDE PRESS

CONTENTS

▼

CONTENTS

THE BLOCKED TRAIL

THE BLOCKED TRAIL

CHAPTER I

EL SOMBRERO

AS he followed the dusty trail at an easy lope around the curve and through the narrow cut, the wind was howling in the ears of Don Esteban Marcos Pulido, and blowing in the wrong direction—so he did not hear the shot.

Nor did he hear the second shot, and the roar of rage that accompanied it. Had he heard, he probably would have pulled up his horse abruptly and refused to continue along the trail until he was sure he would not ride into trouble —which was something Don Esteban always tried to avoid.

Don Esteban Marcos Pulido was not really a Don, and the Pulidos would not have owned him. That was only a high-sounding name he had given himself, and all men knew it, so there was no deception.

He was fat and forty-five, and, like lightning, always followed the path of least resistance.

But he had a good horse and gear, and fair clothes, and always managed to find food for his fat belly—and what man can ask for more?

Now he slouched to one side of the saddle, with his neck-cloth up over mouth and nostrils, and his eyes half closed. He was traveling to the town of Mesaville, on the Border, and it was hot and dusty, and Don Esteban was dreaming of the Mesaville cantina, the interior of which was semidark and cool, and redolent of odors of food and drink.

Something carried by the wind came over the top of the cut and dropped in the middle of the trail a short distance ahead of Don Esteban. The horse he bestrode snorted and shied, and Don Esteban was almost thrown. He became alert, worked for an instant with both reins and rowels, and righted both the horse and himself.

"Son of a coyote!" Don Esteban exclaimed, speaking through his clenched teeth. "Grandson of a ground owl! Have you taken leave of your senses, offspring of a horned toad?"

In the trail ahead, something moved and rolled forward a little as it was tossed by the wind, and the horse snorted and shied again. Then, Don Esteban saw.

"Why, it is a hat!" he exclaimed, aloud and in

surprise. *"El Sombrero!* It also appears to be
an excellent one. And what is it doing here?"

Now his horse saw that it was nothing but
a hat being shifted around by the wind, and
grew calm, and Don Esteban touched with the
spurs and compelled the animal to go closer.
He did not wish to get down out of the saddle
unless it was absolutely necessary, since that
called for a certain amount of exertion. He inspected the sombrero by bending over slightly.

It was, indeed, an excellent article, not something that had been discarded on the trail as
worthless. There was a wide leather band
around it, which seemed to be carved. Don
Esteban decided that it might be worth the effort of getting down into the dust. So he
growled and puffed, and dismounted, and looped
the reins over his arm.

He picked up the sombrero and knocked
some of the fine dust from it. Squinting against
the glare of the sun, he inspected it well. Yes, it
was a good hat! And the leather band—

Don Esteban grunted his surprise and examined the leather band again. It was not
exactly carved. Names had been cut into the
leather, and Don Esteban could read them
easily:

AKERS

BANCORD

WHALEN

LACHMER

Far back in the dim recesses of Don Esteban's fat head, memory cells stirred, though not quite enough.

Akers! Bancord! Whalen! Lachmer!

Those four names had some queer association, Don Esteban knew, but he could not remember what. That troubled him. There was something he should know, and the knowledge evaded him.

He turned the sombrero over and over and read the names on the leather band again, seeking some light in the darkness. But he was compelled to give it up. He had heard something, somewhere and some time, and he had forgotten it. And it was too hot to do much thinking. Anyhow, it was a good hat, and he did not intend to leave it there in the trail.

His horse snorted and shied again, and Don Esteban turned toward the animal with an imprecation rolling from his lips. The wind was still howling in his ears, blowing in the wrong direction, hence he did not hear the hoofbeats of a horse in the soft dust as a rider came around the bend in the trail.

Don Esteban's mount had pulled him along for a distance of ten feet or so before he stopped. Don Esteban, for the moment, was lost in a cloud of fine dust churned by hooves and scattered by the wind.

"Son of a lizard!" cried Don Esteban. "Unspeakable beast with little brains!"

Even the rush of the wind did not kill the voice he heard now, and which seemed to speak into his left ear:

"When you're done insultin' your horse, hombre, maybe you'll give me my hat!"

Don Esteban whirled around as though a sweat bee had stung him on the back of his fat neck. His lower jaw dropped quickly in an expression of surprise. He beheld another horseman leaning forward in his saddle, his forearms crossed over the pommel, and regarding him narrowly.

The first glance told Don Esteban that this man was tall and lean. The second glance took in the rider's face, and revealed a determined chin and piercing eyes. Above the face was a thatch of flaming red hair.

"The wind caught that sombrero of mine and

switched it off my head," the rider explained. "I saw her sail over the rocks and into the cut. Glad you caught it for me."

"It is a pleasure, señor," said Don Esteban. But it was not a pleasure. He had hoped to retain the sombrero.

"Hand it up here," the rider demanded.

Don Esteban handed it up, and then got into his own saddle.

"If you're going to Mesaville, come along," the rider said, as he put the sombrero on his head and adjusted it to his satisfaction. "I'm ridin' that way. Or, maybe you don't want to travel along with me."

"It will be a pleasure, señor."

"Yeah? Don't be too damned sure. Travelin' with me ain't always a pleasure. Sometimes it's right down dangerous."

"I shall do nothing to anger you, señor."

The redheaded one laughed as they started their horses, side by side, through the narrow cut. "I ain't meanin' exactly that I'm dangerous myself, though I sure can be at times. But there's certain hombres like to take a shot at me now and then, and often they shoot wild. One took a shot at me a minute back. He was wild. He won't be wild again."

"Señor! You mean—?"

"I mean he tried to bushwhack me, and missed. But I didn't. You can take a look at him, and see if you know him. I don't."

"If you do not know him, señor, why should he try to kill you?" Don Esteban asked. "Perhaps he made a mistake."

"He knew who he was after, all right! His mistake was in bein' a poor shot, and then stickin' up his head to see whether he'd scored a hit. Horse there behind the rocks, too. We'll take it on to Mesaville."

Don Esteban felt the shivers chasing up and down his spine. Here was trouble—and he did not like trouble. And this redheaded one was so cool and calm about it.

They rode around the curve and out of the cut, and Don Esteban's trail companion pointed to a bunch of rocks off to the left.

"Right there!" he said. "Come along."

Don Esteban was compelled to follow. He had a feeling that this man would resent it if he did not, and he had no desire to arouse the enmity of a man who shot to kill with such little compunction.

They left the trail and rode to the rocks, and the redheaded one pointed. A man was sprawled there, face downward and quite dead. A short distance away, a frightened horse stood tethered to a tree, ears uplifted in question.

"Know him?" the redhead demanded.   He had dismounted and turned the dead man over.

"I never saw him before, señor," Don Esteban said.

"We'll ride on to Mesaville with his horse. Maybe some of his friends will come out and get him."

A few minutes later, they were in the trail again and traveling on toward the town, which was a cluster of brown and white dots in the distance.   The redhead led the horse of the dead man, and Don Esteban rode beside him, scarcely knowing whether to admire or fear.

"What's your name?" the other demanded, suddenly.

"Señor, I am Don Esteban Marcos Pulido."

"I reckon you're a liar."

"Señor?"

" 'Way back in my brain there's somethin' that seems to tell me your name's Pablo—"

"Señor!"   It was a wild cry that Don Esteban gave, one of fear.

" 'S all right with me. I've got a good memory, huh? We'll forget it, hombre. To me, you're Don Esteban and all the rest of it."

"I thank you, señor! Once, when I was but a boy, I did something—"

"Forget it! We all do something. Some of us change our names afterward—and some of us change our natures. It's a lot better, hombre, when you don't have to change anything but your name."

"I presume that is true, señor."

"You're damned right it's true! Me—I haven't changed my name any. But I've changed some, hombre—I've changed! However, that's enough of that!"

"If it is not asking too much, señor, may I know how to address you?" Don Esteban asked. "Since you have not changed your name—"

"I ain't changed it any. But some folks have invented one they use in place of it sometimes. They call me El Sombrero!"

The eyes of Don Esteban grew wide.

"Dios!" he breathed.

CHAPTER II

DON ESTEBAN REMEMBERS

THE memory cells of Don Esteban worked at a furious rate of speed now, so swiftly that they startled him. Fragments became thoughts, and the thoughts became a story.

It was a shock to Don Esteban to find that he was riding at the side of Dan Riley, the man sometimes called "Romance" Riley—but never within his hearing. The story of Romance Riley had traveled up and down the borderline until it was almost a legend.

Dan Riley had been a Texas Ranger. There had been a little affair of robbery and murder, in which several men were concerned. Dan Riley had taken the trail for the purpose of either bringing in the malefactors, else leaving them where they always could be found with dirt above them and boards at their heads.

Dan Riley was young and romantic, and he stopped the night at a certain cantina. The owner of the cantina, Pablo Lopez by name, had

a charming daugher, Carmelita, whose flashing
eyes had intrigued scores of men.

Carmelita Lopez served Dan Riley when he
ate, and carried him drink, sang a bit around the
table, and used her eyes to good advantage.
Nothing particularly wrong in that—Carmelita
was no light baggage.

But Carmelita had ideas, and she had been
born and reared in a district where nine-tenths
of the men were dodging the Law. Her own
father's record was none too white. And she
thought it would be a great thing to outwit a
Ranger.

So she flirted with Dan Riley and coaxed him
to buy a bottle of wine. And when she served
the wine, she slipped into Dan Riley's glass a
pinch of powder. Riley awoke the following
day when the sun was high, to find himself
propped against the wall in the patio, his head
splitting and his tongue thick—and the men he
pursued gone where there was no trail to follow.

The story got out. The Ranger became Romance Riley, and his captain called him in and
told him certain things, the least of which was
that no longer was he a Ranger.

However, he had been a good man, and even
a good man may make a mistake. Hence, a deal

was made. Dan Riley could go forth on his own, and find his men, and bring them in or plant them, as seemed most expedient. When he had done that, perhaps he would be looked upon with favor again.

But the quarry had scattered, and the trail was cold. Dan Riley rode continually, in every direction, always searching, stopping at times to work and replenish his purse. The quest was a joke at first. But iron entered the soul of Dan Riley, and his face grew grim, and men whispered that some day he would meet those he sought. It was no longer a joke. It was a desperate manhunt upon which Dan Riley was engaged.

Akers! Bancord! Whalen! Lachmer!

Those were the men Riley sought. He wore a hat with a wide leather band, upon which those names had been carved, and he had announced that, as he got his men, he would take a hot running iron and sear out the names, one at a time. Always providing that they did not get him first. So, some men called him El Sombrero, as well as Romance Riley.

The four had been living below the Line, playing the bandit game. But Don Esteban knew, from gossip, that they were now in the States again, and evidently Dan Riley knew it, and at last was on their trail. And Don Esteban knew something else, which he believed Dan Riley did not—that Pablo Lopez now operated the cantina in Mesaville, and that his daughter, Carmelita, was there, still making eyes.

"What's troublin' you, hombre?" Riley asked. "You look sick."

"Perhaps it is the heat," said Don Esteban.

"You're a liar again, I reckon. You wilted when I said that some men call me El Sombrero. So you know the story, huh? Oh, you needn't be afraid to say so! It's all right with me."

"I have heard it, Señor Riley, " Don Esteban admitted. "You are stopping at Mesaville, señor?"

"Yeah, I'm stoppin' at Mesaville. Maybe there's a hombre or two around there that I want to see."

"I thought, perhaps, you sought employment with the Señor John Granton."

"Who's he?" Riley asked.

"Recently, he purchased five big ranches, señor, and made them into one. He is the president of a great syndicate. Their holdings fill the valleys on either side of Mesaville."

"I did hear somethin' about that."

"He has been engaging men by the score, señor, and will employ none but the best."

"I ain't got time just now to go punchin' cows," Riley said. "I work when I've got to have money for expenses, but I've got some now. This here John Granton must be a big man."

"He is rich, señor. He has commanding ways. And he has a beautiful daughter, the Señorita Betty—"

"That's enough!" Riley snapped. "If we're goin' to be trail pals, Esteban, you've got to know one thing—never mention women to me! Understand? I hate 'em! I hate the whole tribe of 'em! Never even mention 'em to me to damn 'em!"

"It shall be as you say, Señor Riley."

"You'll live longer, if it is," Riley informed him. His eyes had blazed for a moment, but now his face became inscrutable again. "What do you do for a livin'?" he asked.

"Whoever I may, señor."

"Yeah? You're cussed honest about it. That little affair of yours happened about twenty years ago, didn't it? I've read about it in the records. A drunken brawl, and you knifed another man. Then changed your name and took to the trail. That's been wiped off the books a long time—

nobody gave a cuss for the man you knifed. But my little affair—it ain't been wiped off the books. You know the four men I'm after, don't you?"

"I know their names, señor—I do not know the men."

"Never saw any of 'em?"

"Never, señor!"

"Then they ain't your friends. Good enough! I just wanted to be sure."

"I am *your* friend, señor, if you'll allow it."

"Yeah? I ain't been havin' many friends lately," Dan Riley said. "Sometimes, I wish that I did have one I could trust and talk to. I get damned lonesome. Everybody acts afraid of me, like I was poison."

Dan Riley turned his head a bit and looked out across the parched land, where the black heat waves were dancing. Don Esteban guessed that he was experiencing a spasm of emotion, and did not wish to reveal the fact. It occurred to Don Esteban that he might bask in a sort of reflected glory, if he was the friend and constant companion of this man. There would be a certain amount of danger, it was true, but the danger would be offset by fame.

"Señor Riley, if you wish for a friend, let me be the man," Don Esteban said.

"You tryin' to work on me now, Esteban?"

"Not so, señor! I shall shift for myself always. My friendship will not cost you a cent. I may be of service to you in many ways. I konw this section of the country very well."

"Why do you want to tie up with me, knowin' my story, and realizin' that I'm liable to be in the middle of a bunch of fireworks almost any minute?"

"Honestly, señor, I do not know. I seem drawn to you as a bit of steel to a magnet."

"We'll think it over," Riley told him. "But always remember this—don't mention women to me!"

"I shall remember it, señor."

Don Esteban almost choked as he said it, for he had been at the point of telling Riley of Carmelita's presence in Mesaville. However, there was a way out. Carmelita's father was not a woman, hence Don Esteban could mention him.

"There is now an excellent cantina in Mesaville, señor," Don Esteban said. "It is more than a cantina. There are sleeping rooms around the patio, and good food and drink, and accommodations for horses when one does not wish to turn one's mount into the common corral."

"Fine!" Riley said. "I'll look it over."

"Some months ago, it was purchased by a man who came from elsewhere, and he made certain improvements."

"Who is he?" Riley asked. "Maybe I know him. Funny if I don't! I know every cantina owner along the Border."

The moment had come. Don Esteban seemed to shiver a little, and pretended to be looking at the distant hills. He gulped, and spoke:

"His name is Pablo Lopez, señor."

"Why, damn you—!"

Don Esteban jerked his head around quickly, and saw Riley's face flaming and Riley's right hand reaching for his six-gun. But El Sombrero curbed his ire. His face changed, and then he laughed.

"You're damned clever, Esteban!" he said. "Gave me the tip, and yet—"

"I mentioned no woman," Don Esteban supplied.

"Right! Just this once, Esteban—has this here Pablo Lopez a daughter named Carmelita?"

"It is the same, señor."

"And has she been married, or is she still with her father in the cantina?"

"She is still with her father, señor."

"That'll be enough about her. But, thanks for the tip," Riley said.

They rode on, both silent now, for Riley did not seem to wish to continue the conversation, and Esteban was too wise to start it, not knowing for certain the other's mood. He could not tell whether Dan Riley was dreaming of love or planning revenge.

They were getting close to the town now. For a time they rode down in a depression, and when they mounted to the level again they were within a short distance of the little plaza around which the buildings of Mesaville were grouped.

Riley headed straight toward the cantina, an adobe building which sprawled at the side of the trail. A few men were loitering around it, and a few more wandered around the other buildings, keeping in the shade. Dirty children and mangy dogs played near the adobe huts which formed the residential section of Mesaville.

"It sure ain't much of a town," Riley commented.

"But there are strangers coming and going

continually, señor. This trail runs straight below the Line."

"Yeah! And I understand that some certain hombres have been travelin' it lately—toward the north. That's why I'm here," Riley said. "A man can always get news of travelers at a cantina."

"What is to be done with the dead man's horse?" Esteban asked.

"We'll turn him into the public corral, and see what happens."

They swung away from the cantina and rode to the public corral behind it. Don Esteban remained in his saddle, but Riley dismounted, took the saddle and bridle from the dead man's horse and put them against the corral fence, and turned the animal into the enclosure.

From the near distance, all this was watched carefully by perhaps a dozen men. At the same time, Dan Riley was watching them, seeing if he could identify any of them, estimating them as possible antagonists.

One left the group, and approached. He was a tall, gaunt man with a mean visage. He leaned against the corral and looked at the horse inside, and then at Riley.

"So you've got an extra horse and outfit, huh?" he asked. "Are you wantin' to sell him?"

"Oh, he ain't mine!" Riley explained "I just happened to pick him up out on the trail."

"And him with bridle and saddle on? Maybe you left some hombre afoot out there."

"Oh, I don't reckon so!" Riley told him. "This here horse didn't seem to have anybody to take care of him right, so I brought him in."

"Yeah? He looks a lot like Bill Morgan's horse," the gaunt man said. "Matter o' fact, he is Bill Morgan's horse."

"So that's the name of his owner, huh? You know him?" Riley's voice rasped like a file against metal.

"Yeah, I know him."

"Then maybe you'll be able to locate some of his friends."

"Sure! But what for?"

"Tell 'em that they'll find Bill Morgan about five miles out the trail, just this side of the cut—dead!"

"What's that—dead?" the gaunt man gasped.

"Yeah! He made a mistake, Bill Morgan did—he shot and missed."

CHAPTER III

IN THE CANTINA

WITHOUT answering, the gaunt man turned and strode back to the cantina, where he held speech with the others. Dan Riley got into his saddle, and rode slowly beside Esteban, both watching closely, and neither speaking. They rode to the hitch rail on the shady side of the cantina building, dismounted, and tethered their horses.

The men who had been loitering in the shade outside the cantina had disappeared, and Riley did not doubt that they had gone inside, and were discussing him. He spent a little time slapping the fine trail dust from his clothes, and stretching to remove saddle cramps, and Esteban emulated his example.

"And now, señor—?" Esteban hinted.

"Are you still wantin' to be my friend?"

"It will be an honor, señor."

"You're takin' chances, hombre."

"Only by taking chances does a man win."

"Yeah! But what do you stand to win?"

"Perhaps I, too, grow lonesome at times, and long for real friendship. It is true that I am always well greeted wherever I go, señor. I can play a guitar and sing—"

"Do you ever sing love songs?"

"*Sí, señor!* I know a dozen good ones."

"Yeah? Well, don't you ever sing any of 'em around me," Dan Riley warned. "I'm tellin' you, Esteban! You can sing war songs when you're around me. He-man songs, maybe—but nothin' with a woman in it."

"It is understood, Señor Dan. As I meant to say, I am always cordially greeted. There is food and drink for me. But people look upon me only as an entertaining clown. They do not give me real friendship."

"I reckon I understand," Riley said. "We ought to make a fine pair—a man who's soured on the world, and a clown. We'll see how we get along. Now, we'd better go into the cantina and wash the dust out of our throats."

There was a simple announcement made in an ordinary tone of voice, but there were tremendous possibilities behind it. Riley did not know what he would face when he went into the cantina. He had admitted the shooting of the man

Bill Morgan, and the cantina might be filled with the slain man's friends.

Don Esteban shivered at thought of what might happen. He decided that he would snap the tension, if any existed. He was known here as a jovial man, and he would lead the way into the cantina in a spirit of jollity.

They walked slowly around the corner of the building and approached the entrance, and Esteban managed to get a stride ahead. Through the open door they stepped, to stand quickly to one side, and blink and focus their eyes to the soft semigloom of the building's interior.

Riley adjusted his gunbelt and holster as he peered around the big room, and then started swinging across it toward the head of the bar. But Esteban was before him.

"Greetings, hombres!" he cried. "It is I, Don Esteban Marcos Pulido, come once more among you. Let there be joy and merriment! Bring me wine and a guitar, and I shall sing you songs!"

On another occasion, such an entrance probably would have caused a gale of laughter, and men would have howled at him, and rushed forward to slap him on the back and make him welcome. But now there was an ominous quiet.

About half a dozen men were grouped near the foot of the bar. As many more were standing together on the opposite side of the room. Behind the bar, Pablo Lopez was polishing a glass with a greasy towel.

"Here, you!" Riley snapped at him. He flipped a coin on the board.

Pablo Lopez approached slowly. His eyes were wide, and his face pasty, and he was shaking. He gulped, and licked at his lips as though they had been parched.

"A bottle, and two glasses," Riley ordered. "It's sure been a hot and dusty trail."

"It—it is you, señor!" Lopez gulped.

"Yeah! So you're down in this part of the country now, huh? You move around a lot, don't you, Lopez?"

"Señor! Let me say something, I beg of you. What happened that time—it was not of my doing. I did not know that it was occurring, señor. Not until afterwards was I aware of what actually had happened."

"Am I doin' any talkin' about it now?" Riley demanded. "You seem to be shakin' and shiverin' a lot, for such a hot day. Get out the bottle and glasses. We're about ready to choke."

Though the expression in his face was that of

a man reprieved from death, Lopez said nothing more. He got out the bottle and glasses, and took the coin because Riley insisted, then stood back and watched the pair drink. He glanced imploringly at the men down the bar, and at the others across the room, trying to flash them a message, but they did not understand.

They started from both directions, walking slowly but with evident determination, to converge near where Riley and Esteban were standing. Riley spoke to Esteban from the corner of his mouth.

"Get away from me," he said.

"But, señor, I am your friend! It is my right to help—"

"Get from behind me, fool!"

Don Esteban realized that he was in the line of fire if hostilities commenced. But he refused to show fright. He brought forth materials and began the manufacture of a cigarette, and as he made it he moved aside, yawning, his manner nonchalant. But he was alert and watchful.

Riley began making a cigarette also, standing with his back toward the wall, and facing those who approached. His feet were planted far apart, and his body was well balanced. Those who knew him best would have said that he was in a position to let his right hand drop to his holster with lightning-like speed.

The gaunt man who had visited the corral seemed to be spokesman for the group.

"We'd like to know what you meant, mister, by sayin' that Bill Morgan's dead," he said.

"That's what I mean. Anyhow, the man who was ridin' that horse I turned into the corral 's dead."

"And how did it happen?"

Dan Riley popped the cigarette into his mouth, thumbed a match, and ignited the smoke. He gave a preliminary puff, then bent forward a little, and his eyes met those of the gaunt man squarely.

"I'm tellin' you," Riley said. "I was ridin' along the trail, 'tendin' to my own business, and this gent tried to bushwhack me. He missed— and I let him have it. Then I brought in his horse, which he'd tied to a tree. That's all!"

"Yeah? Maybe it ain't all," the gaunt man said. "Bill Morgan's got some friends here."

"That ain't worryin' me a mite," Riley told him. "I didn't know the hombre, but I know when I'm shot at. And I've got some enemies. This here Bill Morgan was tryin' to do the job for somebody else, I reckon. Maybe somebody afraid to do it himself. But he didn't do it at all proper."

The gaunt man glanced past Riley, to where Don Esteban was standing against the wall and twisting his cigarette in his fingers. "What do you know about all this, Esteban?" he demanded. "You came ridin' into town with this hombre."

It was the first test of the new friendship. Esteban took a step forward and made ready to speak, prepared to stand by his friend whatever the cost. But, as he would have spoken, Riley waved him aside.

"He don't know anything about it at all, except what I told him," Riley said. "I met up with him after the gunnin'. I showed him the dead man, and he said he'd never seen him before."

"And who are you?" the gaunt man demanded. "What's your business? Where'd you come from, and where are you goin'—if you ever leave here at all?"

Dan Riley grinned at him. "Them ain't polite questions—none of 'em," he pointed out. "But I don't mind answerin'. I ain't got anything to hide—like some. My name's Dan Riley."

"*El Sombrero!*" some man exclaimed.

"That's what I'm called by some," Riley admitted. "Since you know that much, I reckon you know my business, too. I'm lookin' for certain gents. And I ain't allowin' anything or anybody to bother me while I'm doin' my lookin'. If that's all, hombres, kindly back away! I'm goin' to that table in the corner, and I want somethin' to eat. You hear that, Lopez?"

He started straight toward them, his arms swinging at his sides, and Esteban followed a few feet behind him, under the impression that he was guarding Riley's back. Those in front gave way to either side, making a lane, and Dan Riley walked through it, not hurrying at all, not nervous in the slightest degree. He eyed those nearest him, and they fell back, and Riley passed them as though unaware of their presence. On to the table he went, and pulled up a stool and sat down.

Don Esteban approached him. "Is there anything I can do to be of service, señor?" he asked.

"Yeah! You can keep away from me for the present," Riley told him. "You're sure cookin' up a pot of trouble for yourself showin' wide and open that you're throwin' in with me."

"But I am your friend, Señor Dan, and your

enemies are mine. If there is to be trouble—"

"If there is, I won't be needin' you," Riley interrupted. "There ain't a man in that bunch for me to worry about—as long as he's in front of me."

CHAPTER IV

DON ESTEBAN retreated with the grace of a hidalgo, though reluctantly, and returned to the end of the bar, where there were dainty morsels of food and a man could eat without paying anything, provided Lopez did not watch him too closely.

The men in the cantina had drawn together again, and were talking in low tones. Riley could not make out what they were saying. Presently, they crowded to the bar and had drinks, then the majority of them departed.

Lopez hurried across to the table.

"Food, and plenty of it!" Riley ordered. "And if the grub's doctored any—"

"Señor Riley, I swear there will be nothing wrong with the food. I shall watch its preparation, and will eat some of it myself."

"I'll be wantin' a room, too, and I want you to put up my horse so's he can have a real feed."

"Then it is your intention to remain in Mesaville?" Lopez asked, his eyes wide.

"Yeah! Until I get damned good and ready to go somewhere else. Why not?"

"There may be danger."

"What of it?" Riley asked. "Danger and me —we're pals."

"But, one man against so many! Those friends of Bill Morgan have gone for a wagon, and will drive out and get the body. After the sunset funeral, they may drink and grow angry."

"Then let 'em get angry at the hombre who set this Bill Morgan to watch for me and bump me out of my saddle. That's the gent for 'em to be angry at."

"And there is also—" Lopez began.

"Are you maybe tryin' to scare me and run me away from your cantina?" Riley interrupted. "You've sure changed some, Lopez. You used to want trade."

"I do want trade, señor—but not trouble in my place," Lopez said. "Those men for whom you are searching—suppose they come here?"

"Nothin' I can think of would please me better'n that, Lopez. Maybe you might be able to arrange it for me, huh? Any of 'em in the neighborhood now?"

"Señor! Do not compel me to take sides in a quarrel," Lopez begged. "I am a man of business, and such must keep friends with everybody."

"Uh-huh! But you won't be a man of business much longer, if you don't answer my questions. It's information I'm after, Lopez. And be damned sure you don't tell me anything but the truth! I've already got one score to settle with you."

The perspiration suddenly popped out on Lopez's greasy face, as his eyes met those of Riley.

"Do not say that, señor!" he begged. "Am I to be held responsible for the tricks of a misbehaving girl? I swear I knew nothing of that until—"

"It's information I'm after, I said. Have I got to wait all day for it?"

"Very well, señor—and I hope this does not cause me serious trouble. It is whispered that one of the men you seek, Sam Akers, is even now working on the big Granton ranch. He is an assistant foreman, and has charge of some men."

Dan Riley sat up straight on his stool, plainly surprised.

"Lopez, are you tellin' me that this here Mr. Granton would give a job to a hombre like Sam

Akers? He's a known outlaw, a bandit, a horse and cattle thief. That's no secret."

"Nevertheless, señor, he is working at the ranch. And the three others you seek—they are expected to arrive soon, and go to work on the Granton ranch also."

"There's somethin' damned funny about that!" Riley declared. "Them four sure ain't noted for work, and it's too late for 'em to reform and get honest. That's sure somethin' for me to think about. And, while I'm thinkin', suppose you go out and rustle me some grub. Hurry it up!"

"At once, señor."

"And when it's ready, let Carmelita come in and wait on me," Riley added.

"Señor!" Lopez exhibited alarm. "You, a strong and brave man, surely would not offer harm to a girl."

"Did I say anything about harmin' her? Maybe I only want to see her eyes sparkle, and hear her sing. Get goin', Lopez!"

It was ten minutes before Carmelita Lopez appeared. She had dressed herself for the occasion. But her face was pale, and fright was in her eyes. She had a sense of guilt in front of Dan Riley. On that day when she had drugged him, she had hidden until he had ridden away, and had not seen him since.

Riley puffed at his cigarette and scrutinized her as she put the food upon the table. He did not speak. Carmelita grew nervous.

"Is there anything else you wish, señor?" she asked.

"That looks like plenty grub," he said. "Yeah, you've got the same pretty eyes! You been leadin' any more men astray?"

"Señor! I did not realize at the time. To me, it was but a joke, to fix a Ranger so he could not get his man!"

"A joke!" Riley extinguished his cigarette and reached for knife and fork. "It got me kicked out of the service, and laughed at from one end of the country to the other. Romance Riley—that's me! I know they're callin' me that. It's cost me almost two years of runnin' around searchin' for certain hombres. It may cost me a lot more yet. Yeah, it was a swell joke!"

"I am truly sorry, señor!" she said.

Riley looked up at her again as he masticated a mouthful of food.

"You are like—blazes!" he said. "You still

think it was a smart trick. I wouldn't be surprised if you've doped my coffee now."

"Oh, señor! If there is anything I can do to atone, I'll do it! I did not dream it would cause so much suffering."

"It also let four thievin' murderers escape," Riley reminded her. "It set 'em up against me, so's I had to shoot a man to-day as was tryin' to kill me—I suppose for them. And there's no tellin' how many more men are goin' to be hurt or killed before it's done—just on account of your little joke."

"Please, señor!" she begged.

"You're a pretty little devil!" Riley complimented. "It's the pretty ones as cause all the trouble."

She stepped closer to the table and talked in whispers. "I'll help you, señor," she said. "The Señor Sam Akers—he comes to the cantina often. And I know that he is coming to-night."

"Akers comin' here to-night?"

"I heard him when he was last here, señor. He rides in from the big Granton ranch to-night, to play poker with some of the men."

"Uh-huh! He'll probably know I'm here, long before he arrives. 'Less I miss my guess, somebody's already ridden out to tell him. But thanks, Carmelita, just the same," Riley said.

"If I learn anything more, señor, I'll let you know. Truly, I am sorry for what I did, and would atone."

"I'll believe that later—maybe," Riley said.

"Do you, wisł me to sing or dance for you, señor?"

"Not right this minute," Riley said. "Perhaps to-night, when the lamps are burnin' and the cool breeze is comin' down from the hills. All I want right now, Carmelita, is another cup of coffee. And, if you dope it, I'll shoot your father before I pass out!"

Carmelita hurried away. Riley finished his meal and made a fresh cigarette. He was puffing at it when she returned with the coffee.

"Who was this Bill Morgan?" Riley asked her.

"I do not know exactly—but he was a friend of Sam Akers."

"I guessed that. And how do you reckon they knew I'd be travelin' this way, and have a man out watchin' for me?"

"I cannot say."

"Is this Don Esteban—and all the rest of it—all right?"

"*Sí, señor!* He plays the guitar and sings—"

"Love songs, I reckon," Riley broke in. "Now, tell me this. Who's the lanky hombre who seemed to be bossin' the crowd around here?"

"That is the Señor Pete Drake. He does not seem to work, yet he always has plenty of money to spend."

"And he's friendly with Sam Akers, huh?"

"Quite friendly with him, señor."

"Thanks! That'll be all for the present, Carmelita."

She stepped close to the table again. "I am forgiven for what I did?" she asked.

"Not yet, you ain't! That'll sure take some forgivin'," Riley said. "'Twasn't like I'd been fool enough to fall in love with you and forget my business. You took an advantage—doped my drink."

"Would it take a fool, señor, to fall in love with me?" she asked, dimpling.

"You might as well cut that out, Carmelita," he said. "I ain't any mark for a woman. You turned me against 'em! They're no good!"

Her face grew serious. "Perhaps, señor, I may prove it otherwise before the end," she said.

"It'll sure take some provin'."

Riley got up from the table and moved slowly

across the room toward the door, and Don Eeste-ban left the bar and followed him.

"Esteban, you'd better decide not to be my friend," Riley said, as they walked toward their horses. "Somethin' tells me that there'll be fireworks to-night, and my friends ain't goin' to be popular."

"But I enjoy fireworks, señor," Don Esteban declared.

CHAPTER V

RÍLEY told him that they would put their horses in Lopez' adobe stable instead of the corral, because diseased stock might have been in the latter. They untied their mounts, and Riley swung up into the saddle. Esteban was busy inspecting a cinch.

Out of the trail and into the town came a thunder of hooves. Somebody gave a strident yell, and other voices echoed it. Riley touched with the spurs and jumped his horse around the corner of the cantina building, to ascertain the meaning of the commotion.

Across the plaza tore a huge black horse, ridden by a girl in riding breeches, who now was standing in the stirrups and fighting to get her frenzied mount under control. Some distance behind her rode a man, unable to overtake the flying black.

On the other side of the plaza there was a sudden chorus of screams. Riley jerked his head around to look. Half a dozen small children

were playing there in the dust, and two frantic
mothers were rushing toward them.

Dan Riley did the obvious thing—gave his
horse the spurs and began racing along a course
that would bring him beside the infuriated black.
He had a glimpse of the white face of the girl
unable to control him. He glanced ahead, and
saw that the women and children would not have
time to get out of harm's way.

A moment later, Riley's mount crashed against
the black, then raced side by side with him.
Riley had an instant's vision of gleaming eyes,
dilated and foam-flecked nostrils. Then his right
hand shot out, and he grasped the reins close to
the bit.

He signaled his own horse, and put all his
weight and strength into swerving the other.
The girl was screeching something that he could
not understand. But it was the children and the
two mothers that caused Riley the most concern.
They were so frightened that they were motionless, stood waiting for destruction to rush down
upon them.

Riley tugged at the reins again, and felt the
black give a little. He guided him in an arc.
They swept so close to the children that they
were deluged with a shower of gravel and dust.

The children and the two mothers were safe, but the black was not conquered.

Riley raced with him past the cantina building, and toward the slope of the hill behind the town. His own horse was tiring, but the black seemed as strong as ever. The girl had ceased fighting since Riley had grasped the reins, and was clinging to the saddle, badly frightened.

Again, Riley swerved the black, and now had him in soft ground, where the going was heavier. He began to tire, as Riley's horse was tiring. Riley tugged and pulled, and turned him back toward the plaza again.

He knew that he had won a victory now. He fought the big black down to a walk, and finally brought him to a standstill a short distance from the cantina. The man who had been pursuing was riding up, and Don Esteban was urging his own mount in that direction.

Now that the danger was over, the girl riding the black started to sway out of the saddle. Dan Riley threw an arm around her quickly.

"Here! Buck up!" he snapped. "There ain't anything to faint about."

"I—I'm all right," she muttered.

"Yeah? You're about ready to keel over, if anybody's askin' me."

"I—want to thank you—those children—"

"Save your thanks!" Riley said, ungraciously. "And after this don't ever ride a horse you can't handle."

That brought her up straight in the saddle. "I can handle him," she said.

"Yeah, I saw you doin' it!"

"Something frightened him, and he bolted. He never did that before. I'll show him that I can handle him. I'll ride him till he drops. I'll get him out on the trail—"

"There you go, takin' it out on the horse," Riley said. "It's just like a woman."

The man came riding up. Riley saw that he was an important-looking individual just past middle age. There was an air of command about him.

"Are you all right, Betty?" he called.

"Yes, father—thanks to this gentleman."

"That was splendid!" her father cried. "Never saw anything better. You know how to handle horses."

"Been handlin' them all my life," Riley replied, smiling a bit.

"I'm John Granton. This is my daughter, Betty. We both owe you a lot for this piece of work."

"That's all right," Riley said. He gathered up his reins. "Glad I happened to be in my saddle and handy. I was tellin' the young lady she shouldn't ever ride a horse she can't handle. He might bolt with her some time when there wasn't anybody around to help."

John Granton threw back his head and laughed, as the girl's face grew red.

"That's good!" Granton said. "Betty's taken more prizes for riding than any girl who ever saw a horse show. She's been just a little too proud about it. Possibly this affair will lessen her conceit."

"Well—I'll be goin'," Riley said. He saw Don Esteban waiting a short distance away.

"Wait, please," Granton said. "Possibly you know of my ranch? I'm always looking for good men. Can't get enough. Mind telling me your name?"

"Dan Riley. I'm a Ranger, but just now I'm on the detached list and with a rovin' commission."

"I was thinking of offering you a job, if you want one."

Riley started to say that he did not want one. But a sudden thought came to him, and he hesitated. Granton was the man who hired Sam

Akers, and who, according to Lopez, was also going to hire the other three men Riley had been pursuing. Surely, there was some mystery about that.

"Well—?" Granton asked.

"Could I speak to you alone a minute, sir?" Riley asked.

"Surely! You're going to the store, aren't you, Betty?"

"Yes, father." She started the black, now thoroughly subdued and willing to be docile, and rode slowly away.

"Mr. Granton, I've been lookin' for some certain men for quite a spell," Riley said. "I let 'em get away from me once. I won't ever stand right with the Ranger force till I get 'em—or see 'em planted."

"I understand, Riley."

"I'm payin' my own expenses till I finish the deal. So I take a job when I've got to have more money. I've got some money now that I saved from my last job—but I might feel like takin' one with you."

"That's splendid! If you'll ride out to the ranch—"

"That is," Riley continued, "maybe. You've

got a man named Sam Akers workin' for you, huh?"

"Yes. Akers is an assistant foreman."

"Mind tellin' me how you happened to hire him? I'm askin' this official, a man might say."

"I see. He came to me with good recommendations from a big ranch over in Mexico."

"Yeah, Akers could do that. You didn't happen to check up on the recommendations, did you?"

"No. I put him to work, and he filled the job. He's a fair man at it. At bit brusque with the other men sometimes—but he knows the work."

"This here job Sam Akers has—that's the job I want," Dan Riley decided.

"But Akers has it."

"He has now," Riley said. "He's comin' to Mesaville to-night, I understand—and he might not get back to the ranch. If he don't, I'll come out and take his job."

"But, I don't understand, Riley."

"You've got one job and two men," Riley said, smiling faintly. "Come mornin', you'll prob'ly have only one man. Either Sam Akers or me won't be able to climb into a saddle."

"So that's the way of it! No way to avoid it?"

"No way. Sam Akers is one of the men I've

been after for quite a spell. He's wanted for murder, bank robbin', horse stealin' and a lot of other things.   Been hidin' out over in Mexico for more'n a year."

"What?" Granton cried. "And I made him an assistant foreman! Prove that, Riley, and I'll kick him off the ranch!"

"I don't reckon that'll be necessary—unless I'm gettin' slow on the draw," Riley returned. "I just wanted you to understand the situation, Mr. Granton. When Sam Akers sees me—and I reckon he knows I'm in town—he'll come shootin'. No chance takin' him in alive. He knows what it'd mean."

"The job is yours, Riley, if you're able to claim it to-morrow."

"Thanks, sir. I aim to make you a good hand. Now, I've got a favor to ask. Do you need a good man to sorter help the cook scrape pots and pans?"

Granton smiled. "Got a pal, have you? Bring him along, and we'll put him to work."

"Esteban, come here!" Riley called.

Esteban rode over to them, acting slightly embarrassed in the presence of the big ranch owner.

"Mr. Granton, this is Don Esteban Marcos Pulido—he says so himself," Riley reported, grinning. "He's the man I'm meanin'—one fine hombre! Esteban, maybe we're both goin' to work for Mr. Granton out on his ranch."

"Work?" Esteban gasped.

"Yeah! It's time you began livin' a useful life. You're goin' to be an assistant cook. That's settled."

It was quite a strain on a new friendship. But Esteban sighed and nodded his assent.

"Anyhow, Señor Dan, it will be much better than punching cattle," he said. "I shall be near the food supply at all times."

CHAPTER VI

"I'M WAITIN' "

INTO the western sky sank the sun, and scarlet and orange banners flamed through the fleecy clouds.

On the hillside behind the town of Mesaville, a score of men were gathered around a crude grave. Bill Morgan was being laid to rest, without much ceremony.

Down at the corner of the cantina building, Dan Riley and Esteban were watching. Riley felt no compunction. He had killed to preserve his own life. Moreover, the man he had killed had been a cowardly assassin lurking in ambush, shooting from behind a ledge of rock.

But that did not alter the situation. The dead man had friends of his own ilk. And Pete Drake, the gaunt one, was their leader. He was a friend of Sam Akers. So Riley watched and listened, and prepared for trouble.

"They are about to come down the hillside, Señor Dan," Esteban said, presently.

"Yeah! If they start anything, you keep out of it."

"Am I not your friend?"

"That don't give you any claim to gettin' yourself filled with hot lead. This here is my own personal fight."

"Would it not be best, Señor Dan, to avoid trouble? You have bigger game in store. Let us walk down by the stable and make sure that our horses are all right."

"You ain't aimin' to tell me that I ought to act like a coward, are you?" Riley asked.

"Everybody knows you are not a coward, señor. You have proved that scores of times. Sometimes it takes courage to walk away."

"You can't dodge trouble, Esteban. A hombre's got to face it and lick it."

Dan Riley stood with his back to the wall, his feet crossed, his arms folded over his chest, smoking a cigarette and watching through narrowed eyes the group descending the hill. Pete Drake, the gaunt one, strode at their head. The men were talking together. No doubt, they had arranged a program.

Inside the cantina, Lopez already had lighted the big kerosene lamps, and the light filtered through doors and windows and mingled with the last flames of the sunset. Dan Riley could be seen easily.

Esteban stood a short distance from him, puffing at a cigarette also, the manner of his puffing betraying the nervous strain under which he was laboring. A thing like this might have been an old story to Dan Riley, but it was a new adventure for Esteban. He was wondering how he happened to be there at all—for he always had been careful to avoid trouble.

The group of men walked at a slower rate as they came to the bottom of the slope and began following a path which led to the cantina. They spread out a little. Though the most of them were armed, none drew a gun. On they came, without speaking, Pete Drake a few feet in front of the others."

"Were you lookin' for me, hombres?" Dan Riley asked the question. That was an old Ranger trick, taking the initiative.

They stopped. Drake came on a couple of strides, and stood with arms akimbo.

"We've been thinkin' as how maybe you didn't give Bill Morgan a fair chance," he said.

"That's sure too bad," Riley commented. "Gents, it ain't pleasant to take human life—but it ain't nice to be shot at, either. Bill Morgan tried to ambush me. Maybe he didn't allow for the wind. Then he popped up his head to see if I'd been hit. Why else should I kill him? I never saw him before."

"We ain't here to listen to any argument," Pete Drake said.

"What are you here for?" Riley demanded.

"We're thinkin' of dealin' with you, Riley."

"Uh-huh! You're goin' to try to succeed where Bill Morgan failed, huh? Same gent goin' to pay the bill?"

"What do you mean by that?" Drake asked.

"You know damned well what I mean, Drake. Bill Morgan didn't have anything against me. We didn't know each other. Somehow, it was learned that I was comin' along the Mesaville trail. And Bill Morgan was sent out to pot me. Now you're all primed to do the same. Who's behind it?"

"I don't know what you mean!"

"I reckon you do," Riley said.

"Let's get him, boys!" Drake cried.

Riley had been waiting for that. He understood the peculiar psychology of hostile groups and mobs. There is a moment when they may be tamed or turned aside. But, move an instant too soon, or delay a second too long, and the chance is lost.

Now, Dan Riley straightened suddenly, and in some strange fashion his six-gun was out of its holster and ready in his hand, and every man in front of him marveled at the speed of the draw.

"I'm coverin' you, Drake!" he announced, calmly. "So go right ahead and give your boys orders to come and get me."

They stood like statues. Riley calmly puffed at his cigarette a moment, then spoke again.

"So you want to get me for killin' Bill Morgan, do you? Why me? Why not get the man who hired Bill Morgan to go out and try to ambush me. He's the hombre who killed Bill Morgan. Why don't he do his own killin'? He prob'ly knows by this time that I'm in town."

"Who are you talkin' about?" Pete Drake asked.

"You know cussed well who I'm talkin' about. I'd admire to meet him face to face, and where there ain't any rocks to get behind."

"Maybe you'll have the chance," Drake cried. "He's on his way to town now. He's comin' to settle with you, Riley!"

"I'm waitin'," Dan Riley said.

CHAPTER VII

AKERS ARRIVES

WITH a shrug of his shoulders, Pete Drake turned aside, and his friends followed him, and they circled around a tree and approached the front door of the cantina, through which they finally passed.

Dan Riley had not moved, except to return his six-gun to its holster when he felt certain that there would be no present hostile move. Esteban slipped through the gathering shadows of the night to his side.

"And what now, Señor Dan?" he asked.

"There ain't anything to do but wait. Drake and his friends are passin' it up to Sam Akers now, and he's the man I want."

"And when he comes, señor—?"

"You can't make plans for a thing like this," Riley said. "If you do they never work out. You've just got to wait till somethin' pops, then be sure you've got your eyes open."

Now, Don Esteban Marcos Pulido had been worrying about something for a few hours, and he decided this was the proper time to mention it. To Esteban's way of thinking it was fully as cogent as Riley's possible duel with Sam Akers.

"Regarding that joke about going to work at the Granton ranch, Señor Dan—what was the significance of that?" he asked.

"That wasn't any joke, Esteban. We're goin' to work there to-morrow, if I'm able to be up and around. I'm to have Sam Akers' job, if he ain't able to 'tend to it himself at that time. And you're goin' to be an assistant to the cook."

"Can it be, señor, that you are serious?"

"You're damned right I'm serious!"

"I cannot understand it," Esteban said. "Why should you take a job punching cattle, when you have money? And why should I—Don Esteban Marcos Pulido—wash pots and pans, and possibly peel potatoes?"

"You ain't scared of work, are you, Esteban?"

"I am not exactly scared of it, señor. But there are many things for which I have a greater admiration."

"Here's the idea, Esteban. Sam Akers' three friends, the men I've been after, are comin' to go to work for Granton. I got that tip to-day."

"Ah! And you wish to be there when they arrive?"

"Yeah! I sure want to be there," Riley said. "Sam Akers is only one on the list. What's he doin' workin' hard on a ranch? And them three bandit friends of his—why do they want to do honest work all of a sudden? Huh? And this man Pete Drake, fussin' around Mesaville, never workin' but always with plenty of money to spend, and him a friend of that gang."

"Señor Dan, as it is often said, a light begins to dawn. I shall peel potatoes and wash pots and pans with pleasure."

"Then that's settled," Riley said, tossing away his smoke. "Now, we'll go into the cantina."

"As you please, señor. I follow where you lead. A man can die but once!" . . .

The cantina was a sort of romantic place at night, with the huge oil lamps casting flickering shadows over the big room, and giving it a touch of softness. The bar was generally busy, and gambling games were on, and there was a tinpan piano which somebody always was pounding.

Strange patrons visited the place, too—men nobody ever saw by daylight. They came in over the trail, stopped at the cantina of Pablo

Lopez to spend a few hours and considerable money, and disappeared into the darkness again. Renegades, wanted men, smugglers, thieves— border rats!

Dan Riley strode into the place with Don Esteban close behind him, and kept near the wall as he made his way toward the rear of the room. His quick eyes found Pete Drake and some of his friends, but they were giving Riley no attention.

They sat at a tiny table, and one of the cantina girls served them with drinks. Carmelita Lopez was beside the piano, singing, while another girl played. Riley squinted his eyes and watched her. This was the girl who had caused his disgrace, caused him to be named "Romance" Riley. The sombrero he wore, with the names carved in the band—that, too, was because of her.

His drink before him on the table untasted, Dan Riley half closed his eyes and considered the past year or so. The land had been laughing at him. Always, following the trail, he had found it blocked. It had got to be a game— keeping Dan Riley away from the men he sought, giving him false information, causing him to ride aimlessly along trails at the end of which he found nothing.

But the hour of triumph for him was near, Riley thought now. He was finally close to the quarry. Sam Akers was coming here to-night. The other three would arrive in a few days, if they did not change their plans. Riley would be face to face with them at last.

It would be a bitter fight, he knew. None of them could afford capture, with ropes waiting for them on one side of the Line and a firing squad on the other. The four were the sort to die with their boots on, and the hard ground their bed.

Somebody stopped beside the table, and Riley glanced up and found Pablo Lopez there.

"Not in my cantina, please, señor!" Lopez begged.

"I don't know what you're talkin' about, Lopez, and I don't believe you do yourself," Riley told him.

"It is being whispered that there is to be a meeting between you and Sam Akers."

"I'm hopin' so," Riley said. "But Akers may not come."

"I happen to know, señor, that one carried word to him, out to the ranch. Akers will come."

Lopez went on, to remonstrate with two who were preparing to quarrel. A whiff of perfume assailed Riley's nostrils. Carmelita was beside the table now.

"So it is that you are a hero, eh, señor?" she said, flashing her eyes at him. "The man who hates women—he is 'Romance' Riley again! He rescues a girl on a runaway horse—and then he puts his arm around her. I saw it, with these eyes of mine."

"I'm bettin' you did," Riley said. "She started to faint, and I held her in the saddle."

"Ah! It is an old game, that fainting. Often have I worked it myself, señor."

"It wasn't any game. She was scared half to death," Riley declared.

"See how you defend her! Can it be that she has struck your heart at first sight?"

"There ain't any woman in the world can strike my heart," Dan Riley declared. "I hate 'em all! You—singin' that love song over by the piano! Damned fools strummin' guitars under windows! It's a pot o' mush!"

Carmelita giggled. "I have heard it said that men of your race make great lovers," she told him. "Perhaps it was a mistake?"

"Far as I'm concerned, it is," Riley said.

"Whose wine are you puttin' dope in to-night?"

Her face clouded. "Never will you forgive me for that!" she said.

"They buried a man up on the hill at sunset. Charge that up to your joke," Riley told her. "And, before the night is through—"

"Señor Dan!" She was speaking in whispers now. "I have been listening to certain men talk. If this Señor Akers comes, and you have trouble with him, stay away from the open window behind the poker table."

"Why?" Riley demanded.

"It is not pleasant, is it, to be shot in the back?"

"So they're plannin' somethin' like that, huh? I thought Akers had guts enough to play square."

"These men were saying that he desired to do so. But it appears that he is important, for some reason. He cannot die just at this time, for that might upset certain plans."

Riley glanced up at her swiftly. "What are you gettin' at?" he asked.

"Why should I explain it to you, when you will not forgive me?" she countered. Then she was gone toward the piano again, to sing another song.

"Fool woman!" Riley growled. "There ought to be a law agin women!"

"That Señor Drake approaches," Esteban whispered. "I am ready to aid you. I can shoot beneath the table—"

"Don't start anything!" Riley snapped. "They've got men planted all around us. It's not Drake I want to quarrel with."

Drake stopped a few feet away, pretended to be looking around the room, and finally met Riley's eyes.

"I'm still waitin', Drake," Riley said.

"Yeah? You won't have to wait much longer, I reckon. Sam Akers is just tyin' his horse to the hitch rail."

CHAPTER VIII

HOT LEAD

SHORT, squat, swarthy, mean of visage and disposition, Sam Akers, despite his long record for crimes and cruelties, was one of the least of the men with whom Dan Riley had to deal. Yet he was an antagonist not to be despised. The man had courage, and could shoot.

He had not come to Mesaville from the Granton ranch alone. Two friends were with him, men of his own ilk. They tethered their ponies to the hitch rail at the side of the building, slapped the dust from their clothes and approached the door. The other two held back and let Sam Akers take the lead.

He hitched up his overalls and chaps, adjusted his gunbelt, swung his six-gun holster around to the position he preferred. A man brushed past him.

"He's at a table in the back of the room, Sam."

"Uh!" Sam Akers grunted his acknowledgment.

Akers waited until a group was passing into the cantina, and went in behind them. He swerved aside and traveled to the head of the bar. He ordered a drink, but allowed it to remain on the bar in front of him untasted.

His narrow, gleaming eyes searched through the room until they found Dan Riley. The latter was leaning back in a chair beside the little table. A cigarette dangled from the corner of his mouth. His body seemed relaxed.

But a thing like that would not deceive an experienced rogue like Sam Akers. Riley really was tensed, he knew, ready to go into action. And he knew Dan Riley's reputation in his Ranger days—a reputation for possessing nerves of steel, for making quick decisions, keeping a mental balance, for hard riding, swift and accurate shooting.

Sam Akers' eyes narrowed more, and a flush suffused his tanned face. Riley was a menace as long as he lived. And there were plans afoot that Akers and some others did not want ruined by the presence on the earth of any one man.

Assassination would not have been difficult, when Akers had so many rogue friends about. But Sam Akers wanted the world to believe that he was capable of conquering Dan Riley single-handed, and fairly.

Akers took his drink. His eyes never left Riley at the table across the room. Riley did not seem to be looking at him at all, seemed oblivious of Akers' presence in the cantina—and that did not fool Sam Akers, either.

A thrill of nervousness seemed to run through the room. One by one, the cantina girls crept away. Carmelita Lopez, scorning to show fear, sat down at the piano, and idly ran her fingers over the keys.

Raucous and strident talk died down gradually. Men moved with a nervous snap. Those near the table at which Dan Riley was sitting were quick to get out of the vicinity. Those near Sam Akers at the bar suddenly believed they had business elsewhere.

Akers was trying to decide what sort of move Riley would make, was waiting for it. He did not want to be the aggressor, but neither did he want to be caught off guard. Riley gave no sign, though he looked straight at Akers once.

Sam Akers began to feel a measure of nervousness himself, but fought it off. If it was to be a waiting game, he could play it that way. But he would not wait too long.

Now it was almost dead quiet in the cantina. Poker chips clicked as players handled them, a murmur of voices swept through the room. There were no other sounds. Behind the bar, Lopez was ready to drop to safety if trouble began.

Men sauntered out the front door—and wiped the perspiration from their faces as soon as they emerged into the zone of safety. Each second they expected to hear a blast of gunfire, perhaps the cry of a mortally wounded man.

And then—the tinkling of the old piano, and a girl's voice in song!

Carmelita Lopez wrecked the nervous strain of the cantina. The song grew in volume until it filled the big room. Men began talking loudly again, and moved around. But Dan Riley remained leaning back in his chair, the cigarette dangling from his lips, his appearance that of a man half asleep.

Sam Akers growled a curse and started along the bar. Other men got out of his path, avoided his vicinity. Watching Riley from the corners of his eyes, Akers passed him and continued along the bar.

He turned away, toward the piano. Carmelita was just ending her song. Sam Akers leaned against the end of the piano, so he could talk to her and watch Riley at the same time.

"Hello, sweetheart!" Akers said.

She twisted away from him as he tried to grasp her arm.

"Coy to-night, huh?" Sam Akers spoke in a voice that all in the room could hear, for suddenly it had grown quiet again. "I reckon I understand, Carmelita. An old flame o' yours is here to-night, somebody told me."

"It is my wish, señor, that you do not bother me," Carmelita said. "I have a headache."

"You've just been singin', so it can't ache very bad. I know—you're afraid he'll get jealous o' me. Has he been buyin' any wine to-night?"

Some in the room gasped at that, knowing the story of the drugged wine that had resulted in Dan Riley's professional disgrace. But Riley gave no sign that he had heard. He teetered in his chair, and, always on guard, struck a match and lighted his cigarette again.

"Do you ever hear from Romance Riley these days, Carmelita?" Sam Akers demanded, in a loud voice. "I understand he's right down peeved at you for what you did. He was chasin' four naughty hombres, and forgot what he was doin'."

Nor did that thrust bring any response from Dan Riley. He took the cigarette from his mouth, while all in the place watched him—and yawned.

Sam Akers growled a curse. Carmelita got up and started away from the piano, and Akers let her go. Riley had yawned! The red badge of rage decorated Akers' face again.

He hitched up his belt and left the piano, starting on a course that would carry him past Riley's table. Men moved swiftly out of the way again, got out of every possible line of fire.

At the table, Riley, from the corner of his mouth, and with scarcely any movement of his lips, spoke to Esteban: "Get goin'!"

"But, señor—" Esteban protested.

"Get away! Else maybe we won't either of us work for the Granton ranch."

Don Esteban got out of his chair slowly and turned aside, being very particular not to hurry about it. He wanted to remain, but he was a man to obey orders. And he judged that Dan Riley knew what he was about.

Riley did not shift his position, apparently, but his right hand dropped down to his waist, and he hooked his thumb into his belt. Sam Akers saw that slight move and knew its significance. Riley was on guard, strictly so. He could snap his six-gun out of its holster as readily as Akers could get out his own weapon.

But Akers had started this, and the eyes of all in the room were upon him. He could not turn back now, or his prestige would be gone forever. He walked slowly and deliberately toward the table, his boots thumping the floor with a hollow sound.

A few feet from the table, he stopped. Dan Riley was regarding him from the corners of his eyes.

"I understand you've been lookin' for me, Riley," Sam Akers said.

"Yeah! I've been lookin' for you for quite awhile," Riley replied. "Down in Mexico for a spell, wasn't you—playin' bandit?"

"And what did you want me for?" Akers demanded.

"Me? Three murders and about a score of stealins'."

"Well, here I am!"

"So I see," said Riley. "A little heavier. Must be gettin' good, regular eats."

"I can't say you've been improvin' any," Akers sneered. "Well, what are you goin' to do about it, Riley?"

"About what?"

"You've been lookin' for me, and here I am."

"I'll take care of you when I get around to it," Riley said. "There ain't any rush—now that I know where you are. And you've got some friends comin' soon, I understand."

"If it's a waitin' game you're playin', I can match you at it, Riley. My nerves are as good as yours."

"We'll see, Akers."

Sam Akers' blood was boiling. He felt that Riley was getting the best of this encounter, and that infuriated him. He felt an urge to go for his six-gun and have a decision. But something seemed to hold his hand. He sensed that such a move would mean his instant death.

"After lookin' so long and so hard for me, you don't seem to be any too damned excited about findin' me," Akers said. "Maybe you've changed your mind about what you were goin' to do, huh?"

"Not any!" Riley said.

"I reckon it'd be safe if I turned my back on you and walked to the bar."

"Sure!" Riley replied. "I ain't any Bill Morgan. I don't do my shootin' from ambush —and I don't hire out my gun."

"What are you meanin' to insinuate, Riley?"

Riley eyed him squarely. "I'm meanin' to say that the old sayin' is correct—if you want somethin' done right, do it yourself."

Sam Akers' eyes grew narrow and blazed. He thrust out his chin. His hands became fists at his sides. He fought to regain control of himself. Enraged, and with Dan Riley as cold as ice, Akers knew he would be at a terrible disadvantage.

"I ain't goin' to stand here gassin' with you all night," Akers said, finally. "I heard you were so damned eager to see me that you'd been trailin' me all over. And here I am, and you ain't doin' anything about it."

"I'll get around to that," Riley told him.

Sam Akers glared at him a moment—and then deliberately turned his back. Slowly, he started across the big room toward the bar, his hands swinging at his sides. And suddenly he stopped, lurched to one side, and whirled. His six-gun came from its holster.

"Damn you, Riley—!"

Two guns barked, a fraction of a second between them. Sam Akers lurched again and swayed forward, half turned, and crashed to the floor. Dan Riley was still sitting in the chair at the table, with the cigarette still dangling from the corner of his mouth.

"I knew he was goin' to try that," Riley said. "I was watchin' his face in the mirror on the back bar across the room."

Now that it was over, Riley got to his feet, while some of those in the cantina rushed to the fallen Sam Akers. Riley beckoned to Esteban, who hurried to him.

"Do me a favor, Esteban?" Riley asked.

"At any time, señor!"

"Go to the barn and get that runnin' iron out of my stuff. I want to heat it up, and burn a name off my leather hat band."

CHAPTER IX

THE TRAP

DON ESTEBAN MARCOS PULIDO, now that Sam Akers had been removed, came to the realization that, for the first time in his life, he was to hold down a job. The thing was a distinct shock. There was a brief moment when he had the idea of telling Dan Riley that their bond of friendship must be severed, that he would face perils with his new friend, stand at his back in combat, starve with him and face the rigors of the climate with him—but would not work for him or anybody else.

But Don Esteban thought better of it soon. He was a fatalist—and what was to be would be. Moreover, he had honor of a sort and was not without courage. Explorers had gone into strange countries and lived to tell the tale, and so would he.

But there was a certain amount of reaction. Don Esteban found friends, and sang for them, in return for which singing he received gratis certain strong liquors which loosened his tongue.

He pitied his lot to the extent of telling about it. He did not tell much, but it was enough. He related that Dan Riley was going to work for the Granton ranch, and that he, Don Esteban Marcos Pulido, was going with him, and that they would ride out in the morning.

Plenty of people heard the yarn, and it was relayed to others. And, after a time, it came to the ears of Pete Drake, who called some others into a conference. After that, Drake and his friends kept away from Riley, offered him no affront, did not even favor him with a glare.

More men came into the cantina off the trail, men who often glanced behind furtively. Business increased. Riley tired of the din, and decided that he would get some sleep. He said as much to Esteban, for whom he had arranged for accommodations.

He left the cantina and went out into the patio, which now was flooded with moonlight, and walked along beneath the arches toward the room which had been assigned to him by Lopez. He was cautious and alert, as always, though he did not anticipate an attack at this time.

Riley turned in. He did not use the cot, but left a roll of blankets upon it to resemble a sleeping man, and took more blankets and made himself a pallet in a corner of the little room. But he could have used the cot. For, when the first streak of dawn found him awake, nothing had happened to mar his slumber.

He bathed face and hands in the pool in the patio, went into the cantina, and ordered something to eat. The big room had a sort of "morning after" appearance now. Lopez was still behind the bar, and Riley wondered when the man ever slept. And Carmelita brought the breakfast.

"So you are going to work for Señor Granton," she said. "Don Esteban told me. That will be a fine job, eh, señor? All day long you can rescue girls who do not know how to ride horses."

"Your jealous streak's showin' this mornin'," Riley told her.

She tossed her head. "Jealous? Of a girl with yellow hair and blue eyes? But of course her father is a rich man."

Riley grinned. "Never thought of that," he said.

She faced him defiantly. "Señor Dan, are you going to forgive me?" she demanded.

Riley's face sobered as he met her direct gaze.

"You know what happened here last night," he said. "If you had not played your little trick, Sam Akers would not have made me kill him. I could have taken him alive that night you drugged my wine. I had the plans all made, had a trap arranged."

"Oh, señor!" she sobbed.

"It's nothin' to worry about now," he assured her. "It's done. Far as I'm concerned, I'm forgivin' you for all the trouble you've caused me."

"Thanks, Señor Dan!" She flashed a smile at him. "Perhaps, some day, I can repay you in some manner. And now, if you are going to work at the Granton ranch, you will be coming into Mesaville often—si?"

"I reckon," Riley said. "It's the only town for a lot of miles."

"And you will come to the cantina?"

"It's the only place here a man can get anything to eat and drink."

"And you will always watch for Carmelita?"

"I knew cussed well you were leadin' up to somethin' like that," Riley said. "You clear out o' here, now. I don't want anything to do with no women! I hate 'em!"

"Even those with yellow hair and blue eyes, señor?"

"Any color hair and any color eyes—I hate 'em! Get me some more coffee!"

Don Esteban appeared a moment later, having breakfasted at the hut of a friend. He had the horses ready for the trail. So, just as the sun was peeping up over the hills to the east, they started out, turning into the north trail and going along at an easy pace that would eat up the miles.

They took deep draughts of the bracing air and watched the buzzards wheel a cloudless sky as they looked for their morning meal. Long before they came to the ranch, they knew, the black heat waves would be dancing, and the merciless sun would be broiling them.

They came to a hill where the trail was only gravel and sand and the footing treacherous, and allowed their mounts to make their own way.

"Broken country from here on, señor," Esteban said.

"Yeah? Valley on the other side, huh?"

"*Si, señor!* The headquarters ranch house is but a short distance from this end of the valley.

Two hours, say, and we shall be there. And then—the pots and pans!"

"Broken country," Riley said. "Ambush country!"

"You are expecting trouble, Señor Dan?"

"I'm always expectin' trouble, and I generally find it."

"Those other three—possibly they have not yet arrived."

"I reckon not," Riley said. "They'll be driftin' in. I don't think the death of Akers will keep 'em from comin' to the ranch. There's somethin' goin' on behind all this, and I don't think Akers' death 'll stop it."

"And what am I to do, señor, at the ranch, in addition to my work in the kitchen?"

"Just keep your eyes and ears open, Esteban. I'll be livin' in the bunk house, and you'll prob'ly do the same. We'll get plenty chances to talk. This season of the year, the men 'll be scattered out on the range a lot, comin' and goin'."

"Making more chances for ambush, señor?"

"Yeah! It'll be no time for me to go ridin' against the skyline, I reckon."

They came to the top of the hill and made

better speed, for they wanted to get to the ranch before it got too hot, and get settled. The trail wound across the flat like a dirty yellow ribbon, and the ground on either side was even. No chance for an ambush there.

But there was a distance of only two miles of that, and then the road went once more into broken country, where jumbles of rocks were on either side, with the trail curving through them so that a man could not see very far ahead.

Dan Riley loosened his six-gun in its holster, and his eyes were busy scanning the rocks. There was nothing to indicate danger. Here, he was riding ahead, and Don Esteban close behind him. Around a curve they went, where the trail was narrow, and frowning rocks were on either side. Nothing happened there.

Then they could look ahead and see the broad valley through the cut, and knew that soon they would be out in the open, and only a short distance to go until they came to the big ranch-house. It was hot in the cut, but there would be a breeze when they got out into the open again.

In the shade cast by the last jumble of rocks, they stopped to let their mounts rest, and to smoke before continuing the journey. Their cigarettes finished, they put up their neckcloths and started on.

Suddenly, they were on a flat again, save that here and there were little rocky buttes half covered with dry grass and weeds. And, as they rode out, a rifle cracked, and a bullet sang past within inches of Dan Riley's head.

"Knew it!" Riley barked.

He swerved his horse abruptly, as another shot came and another bullet almost struck him. Esteban had swerved his horse also. Now they used the spurs and dashed forward, and turned to look back.

Up in that last jumble of rocks, a tiny wisp of smoke betrayed the location of their foe.

"Let's go get that hombre," Riley suggested, as he pulled up his horse and Esteban stopped beside him. "That was a rifle he used—could tell by the bark."

"And we have nothing but six-guns, señor."

"Yeah, we have somethin' else—we've got guts. Me, I'm tired of bein' shot at from behind rocks. It's time to do somethin' about it."

"You did something but yesterday, señor, concerning that Bill Morgan. As you say, Señor

Dan. I am but a follower where my leader leads."

"He's in one fine position," Riley said, as they urged their horses off the trail and started to circle back. "But maybe we can get close without bein' popped off. Keep to cover as much as you can."

They rode in zigzag fashion, now with speed and now slowly, rode behind hummocks and rocks, did everything possible to disconcert the aim of the enemy. Another shot came, but not even near enough to cause them a feeling of discomfort.

Now Riley grew cautious, and Esteban fell back behind him. No more bullets had been sent toward them. Either the enemy had decided to ride for it, else was waiting for them to come within better range, and Riley somehow believed the latter.

They rode out of a depression, their intention being to make for a hillock, get behind it and circle it, and so come to a place from which they could make a rush at their man. But, as they emerged, Esteban gave a shout, and Riley turned quickly to look.

From two directions, mounted men were

bearing down upon them, shooting as they came. And the foe up in the rocks opened up with the rifle again.

"It's a trap!" Riley cried at Esteban. "Follow me!"

CHAPTER X

POUNDING HOOVES

RILEY turned his horse and began racing across the rough, uneven ground, risking the danger of the horse stumbling and himself being thrown. Esteban followed him, only turning once to fire a single shot at those who pursued.

Riley was leading the way toward a tiny butte studded with rocks, elevated some twenty feet above the surrounding country. There were three men pursuing, and now the one who had been using the rifle also came into view, mounted, to join the pursuit.

Four to two, and no chance to run for it, even had Dan Riley wished to do so. Neither Riley's horse nor Esteban's was noted for excessive speed; the mounts of their pursuers probably were as good. And they were still some three or four miles from the Granton ranch house.

Around the shoulder of the little butte, Riley led the way. He jerked his horse to a skidding stop, and Esteban, watching for just that, followed his example. They sprang out of the saddles, trailed the reins, began climbing

Before they reached the top and found barricade behind the rocks, they could hear the thundering hooves of the horses their pursuers rode. Riley dropped behind a rock and got out his six-gun. He put a bullet past the head of the leading horseman, and the three stopped their headlong rush and scattered. The fourth man had not caught up with them, but was approaching rapidly.

Riley fired again, and missed. Beside him, Esteban flattened himself on the hard earth and tossed his sombrero aside. He examined his six-gun methodically and prepared for battle.

"They're huntin' cover," Riley said.

The three had dismounted, trailed their reins, and were getting behind rocks and clumps of brush. The fourth man came up to them, shouted something Riley and Esteban could not catch, and circled toward the left.

"Got us surrounded," Riley said. "Prob'ly got rifles, too. No sense wastin' cartridges, Esteban. Hold your fire until you're pretty sure you can hit somethin'."

"Four of them—they flatter us, señor."

"That Pete Drake is one of 'em," Riley said. "He was hooked up with Sam Akers, all right.

Hooked up with some others, too, I'm thinkin'. Have to see about it, when we get out of this."

Bullets began peppering the rocks, ricocheting, singing off across the country.

"They are playing music for us, señor," Esteban offered.

"Yeah! Fine tune! No damned love song, though, like you'd play on a guitar."

"If they should try to rush us—"

"I'm hopin' they do," Riley interrupted. "Get 'em within six-gun range, and we might be able to do somethin'."

He risked a quick reconnaissance. He could spot three of the men easily by smoke from their guns, but did not see the fourth. A bullet sang past his head, and he dropped down behind the rock.

Then Riley crawled to the other side, and risked a look there. Esteban heard him fire twice, rapidly, heard also a muttered imprecation.

"What is it, Señor Dan?" Esteban asked.

"That fourth skunk was tryin' to get our horses and set us on the ground."

"Did you get him, señor?"

"Nothin' serious. Hit him, though. Saw

him reel in his saddle and clutch his left shoulder. Chased him away, anyhow. He's makin' for the others."

With death singing around them, Esteban had a complaint. "Señor Dan, it is hot up here in the rocks," he announced. "It will grow hotter."

"Yeah—maybe in more ways than one."

"And our canteens are on our saddles."

"I've got some extra ammunition in a saddlebag, too," Riley said. "But they're in a position to pot us if we try to get to the horses."

"Then, señor, we are to remain here dodging bullets, and broil?"

"You're so fat you'd fry," Riley said.

He risked another look, and emptied his gun, then dodged down behind the rock to reload, while the enemy expended ammunition recklessly. Esteban crawled to the other side and peered down at the horses.

"I could enjoy a drink of water, even such warm water as is in our canteens," he remarked.

"Stay where you are!" Riley snapped. "They'd put a couple of slugs of lead in your hat, then my army'd be cut in half. We're outnumbered bad enough as it is."

"Something must be done," Esteban said. "It

is bitter that such scum can make us hole in and sweat in this fashion. A feeling of insult comes to me."

"If you die here, you won't have to scrape pots and pans."

"Cleansing pots and pans is a worthy occupation. I hope to do it often," Esteban said.

A glancing bullet whipped past him, and he tried to squeeze down behind the rock. Riley changed position and dared another look.

"They're comin' nearer," he said. "Creepin' up on us, and keepin' to cover while they're doin' it."

"Let's try for the horses, señor."

"Slim chance, doin' that. But maybe you're right. They can keep us holed up here for hours, and may get us in the end."

"If somebody would only come along the trail and hear the battle—"

"Prob'ly pay no attention to it, if they did," Riley told him. "Wind's blowin' the wrong way to carry the sounds. Puffs of smoke 'd look like swirls of dust."

"You are very discouraging," Esteban complained.

"I warned you not to come playin' partner

around me, didn't I? Told you there'd be fireworks and trouble."

"It is worth it, señor, to be your friend."

Another fusillade came from the enemy, and
bullets splattered around the rocks. Riley put
up his head quickly, in time to see three of the
four rushing forward after they had fired, seeking new cover nearer the base of the butte. He
emptied his six-gun.

"Nicked one of 'em," he said, as he reloaded.
"That makes too o' the four nicked. But they
can still shoot."

He crawled to a new position and took a look.
There might be a chance to get at the horses, but
it would be running a risk to try it. He put it
up to Esteban.

"Want to try to ride for it?"

"It is better than remaining here," Esteban
said.

"Get ready, then. Wait till they send another
volley at us, and we'll crack back at 'em, then
make a dash. And I sure hope luck's with us!"

The volley came as he finished speaking, and
they lifted their heads to find two of their foes
changing position again. A third was some distance back, probably the wounded one. The
fourth was a still greater distance away.

"Now's the time!" Riley said.

They sprang down from the rocks, fell and scrambled, rolled through the dust and across the rough gravel. At the base of the butte, they bent low and raced for their mounts.

Guns cracked and flamed as their retreat was discovered. But they caught up their mounts and swung up into their saddles. Straight away from the butte they raced, toward a depression which would give them some cover.

Two of their foes mounted and followed, riding near together. A third came along behind. The fourth did not pursue.

Riley glanced back, and saw that Pete Drake was one of the two nearest. If the third man could be distanced, and the odds thus made even, it would be possible to turn and fight it out. Something like that was in Riley's mind. He did not like this running away.

Esteban was riding parallel with him, following Riley's leadership as to direction. Those behind were firing frequently, in the hope, possibly, of scoring a lucky hit.

Riley waved toward what seemed to be a trail running toward the distant ranch house. Esteban turned toward it with him. They jumped a gully, turned into the trail, and raced on.

And then disaster came, at a moment when Riley was hoping for a chance to stop and put up a fight, now that the third man was far behind.

He saw Esteban's horse stumble, stagger, reel, fall. Esteban shot over his head to strike with force against the hard ground. Riley pulled up his mount, swerved, rode off to one side. His six-gun came out, and he opened fire.

In the face of his fire, the two pursuers, Drake and another man, pulled up their horses also, and tried to find cover. But there was scant cover beside the trail. Riley urged his horse to speed, rode like a fiend back to where Esteban had fallen, where his horse was trying to struggle to his feet.

A bullet sent Riley's sombrero flying from his head. He fired in reply, but missed. The third rider, he saw, was coming up and soon would be able to join in the fight.

Riley had no delusion about what was happening. These men were out to kill him, because he was a menace to their plans. They had failed the day before, had failed a short time ago at the mouth of the little pass. And so eager were they to accomplish their work that they had followed this near the Granton ranch house, with men working out on the range.

He skidded his horse to a stop beside Esteban, who was getting to his feet. Esteban's horse did not have a broken leg, as Riley had feared, but he was no good now as a mount. He limped away from the trail.

"Up behind me!" Riley barked, as he fired again at the man nearest.

"Ride and leave me, señor! They will not harm—"

"Up!" Riley commanded.

He fired again, wheeled his horse, made it possible for Esteban to mount on the side away from the enemy. But Esteban swayed and tottered, and let go of the saddle. He was still half dazed from his fall.

Drake and the other man were circling, starting to ride forward. Riley knew their intention—to get close enough to make sure of their work. He snapped shots at both of them, failed to score a hit.

Esteban had tottered away, and had dropped to the ground to sit holding his head in his hands. Riley could not remain there inactive, a target for three guns. And he did not want to ride away and leave Esteban.

It was a problem—but it was solved. Down the trail from the opposite direction roared the thunder of pounding hooves.

CHAPTER XI

A JOB REFUSED

HIS first glance revealed to Dan Riley a huge black horse charging along like some wild monster bent on destruction. Riding him was the girl he had seen the day before in Mesaville—Betty Granton. Behind her raced three cowpunchers.

Drake and his companions turned and made a run for it. The Granton cowboys shrieked a challenge and started in pursuit. Betty Granton stopped the big black as soon as possible, turned and came back.

Riley had dismounted and hurried to Esteban's side. But Esteban was not injured beyond the shock of the fall. He got to his feet, shaking his head, as the girl came up.

"If you'll take care of him, miss, I'll be chasin' them critters," Riley said.

"The boys are giving them the run, Riley," she replied. "You're not needed. What happened?"

"Four men jumped us back at the pass—ambushed us. We had to make a fight. Then we tried to get to the ranch, but Esteban's horse fell."

"Know the men?" she asked.

"I know one of 'em by name. Didn't get a chance to see the others very well."

"Which man did you recognize?"

"You wouldn't know him, I reckon. He hangs around Mesaville a lot, I understand. I'll 'tend to him, later."

"Tell me his name," she said, her tone one of authority. "You can settle with him whenever it pleases you, and I'll not bother—"

"I ain't used to havin' folks bother in my business."

"Not very polite, are you, Riley?"

"I beg pardon! But I—I don't like women."

She laughed a little. "I don't, either—not many women," she confessed. "They're a queer lot. I've a reason for asking you that man's name, Riley. Was he Pete Drake?"

"You seem to know," Riley said.

"I thought as much." A serious look came into her face. She turned to look at the fleeing men. The Granton cowpunchers were getting a lot of fun out of the chase. They were empty-ing their six-guns at the fugitives, probably with no expectation of hitting the target under those conditions. But they gave speed to the flight.

"Let's be getting home," she said. "What's your friend's name?"

Riley grinned. "He's Don Esteban Marcos Pulido."

"Don Esteban can get on his own horse and come along slowly. The boys will pick him up."

"Maybe I'd better wait and come along with him," Riley said, in sudden panic. He was commencing to be afraid of this girl.

"Nonsense! I want to talk to you."

Riley mounted as Esteban got into his own saddle, having ascertained that his mount had suffered nothing worse than a sprained leg. Betty Granton started slowly along the trail, then stopped and waited for Riley to catch up with her.

"I feel that I can trust you, Riley," she said. "I've heard a lot about you—know your story. You needn't blush! You'll square everything by getting your men, I'm sure. Got Sam Akers in town last night, didn't you?"

"Yes'm. It was a case of that or him get me."

She glanced at his hat, which he had recovered and now was wearing.

"One name burned off," she said. "And there are three more."

"When they've been burned off, I'll get me a new hat band."

"Know where those three men are, Riley?"

"Not right at this minute, miss."

"Don't call me 'miss'. Call me Betty. All the punchers do. So you don't know where they are at this minute. But you think you'll be running across them soon, don't you?"

"I wouldn't be a bit surprised."

"Don't you really happen to know that they're coming here to work for Dad?"

"Well, I heard that," Riley confessed.

"They are. I happen to know. Bully Bancord and Hank Whalen, as they're known, will be here to-morrow or the next day. And the other, the one they call 'Dude' Lachmer, will arrive in about a week."

"It seems right down funny to me that them hombres would want to work at honest jobs," Riley said. "I know a lot about 'em, and I can't understand it."

"Possibly I can explain it to you—later," she said.

"I'd sure admire to have it explained."

"Can I trust you, Riley?"

"I reckon."

"There's something going on, and it's got my Dad worried. Whatever it is, I think he got into it without knowing. He thought that Sam Akers was all right. And these other three—"

"That's easy," Riley said, as she hesitated. "All your father's got to do is say he don't want 'em to work—and leave the rest to me. They're all wanted men. I've got a right to arrest 'em and take 'em in—or the other thing, if they resist."

"We'll talk about it later," she said.

Then they rode for a time in silence. She did not seem to wish to continue the conversation, and Riley was glad. He was looking over the home ranch, inspecting the buildings and fences and general equipment.

Riley knew ranches, and his eyes glowed as he looked at this layout owned by a big corporation. You could do things with money!

"Who's the foreman?" he asked, abruptly.

"Bill Kline," she replied, smiling at him. "He's really a sort of superintendent, and has several assistant foremen under him. You're to be one, aren't you?"

"That's the plan," Riley said. "Where'll I

find this Mr. Kline? I'll have to report that I'm ready for work—Esteban, too."

"There's a special little building for his office," she said. "I'll show you when we get there."

Now they came to a shady lane and went along it at an easy lope. Riley was admiring the big black she was riding, and he remembered something.

"I'm right down sorry for what I said yesterday—that you didn't know how to handle horses," he said.

"It's all right, Riley. Didn't look like I did, yesterday, did it?"

Riley grinned. "Oh, I've had 'em bolt with me, too," he said. "Any horse is liable to get a crazy spell. Horses are like wo—"

"Go on and say it, Riley. Horses are like women that way—liable to get crazy spells. You certainly don't like women. Possibly, some day, one will make you change your mind about the sex."

"If one ever does," Dan Riley said, "she'll have to be a humdinger!"

They were approaching the big ranch house, which was no less than a mansion. Betty Granton pointed off to the left.

"That little building with the two trees in front of it," she said, "is the office. You'll find Mr. Kline there, probably."

"Thanks! I'll find him. Esteban will be comin' along pretty quick."

"And I may want to talk to you, Riley, about what's troubling me, and Dad. I feel that I can trust you. You've been a Ranger—and will be again."

"Am now, but under a cloud, as a man might say. Got authority."

"That's splendid. You may need to exercise it," she said.

"What's it all about, anyhow?"

"Later, Riley." Her pretty face had clouded again. "You'd better see Mr. Kline now."

She wheeled her horse and rode toward the veranda steps of the big house, and Riley went toward the office. He dismounted and tied his horse, and went up to the door and knocked.

"Come in!" a gruff voice called.

Hat in hand, Riley opened the door and entered. He found a large room filled with desks and filing cabinets, and a man sitting behind the biggest desk chewing an unlighted cigar. Hard as granite, that man, Riley decided.

"I'm lookin' for Mr. Kline," Riley said.

"I'm Kline."

"My name's Riley. Mr. Granton told me to report for work to-day, me and my friend, Esteban—"

"Yes, I know." Kline took the cigar from his mouth and got up. He was a massive man. "But Mr. Granton's changed his mind."

"How's that?"

"There's nothing here for you, Riley. Sorry! You and your friend can ride back to Mesaville."

CHAPTER XII

SOMEBODY IN A HURRY

DAN RILEY was so used to meeting the unexpected that it seldom shocked him. In his life, an emergency always had been just around the corner. But this was something of a blow.

"I don't understand," Riley said. "Mr. Granton told me—"

"I know," Kline interrupted. "But there are swift changes often in the affairs of a big company."

"I reckon a small man like me in an assistant foreman's job wouldn't mix up much in company business."

"There's no argument, Riley."

"I ain't tryin' to argue, Mr. Kline. I'm just sayin' that it's funny. I ride out here with my friend, Esteban, to take jobs, and you say there ain't any for us. It's a long way to Mesaville, and we had a little brush with some hombres, and Esteban's horse is hurt so he can't travel fast."

Riley thought that he saw Kline's eyes glow at that statement, but could not be sure.

"Sorry about the horse," Kline said.

"Well, if there ain't jobs, there ain't. Funny thing is that I told Mr. Granton I wasn't right down particular whether I took a job or not, and he seemed right tickled when I said I would."

"Changed his mind," said Kline.

"Could I maybe see Mr. Granton?"

"Afraid not. He's quite busy at the house."

"Uh-huh! How about Esteban leavin' his horse here and usin' a ranch horse to get to town?"

"We don't let strangers have our horses. Blooded stock and all that."

"Yeah? Esteban's horse is a good one, and he's a good rider. You ain't got any objections, I reckon, if we go to the cook shack and get us a little snack."

"We're not running a hotel here, Riley," Kline told him. "You and your friend better get back to Mesaville."

Riley's eyes grew narrow, and his face flushed beneath its protecting coat of tan. No ranch he ever had known refused to feed visitors. Hospitality was always extended. The loan of

a horse would not have been refused anywhere
else, as far as Riley knew.

But he remembered that this huge affair was
operated by a wealthy syndicate, and that they
ran on a strictly business basis. The operating
agents were not westerners with the western
spirit.

"All right!" Riley said. "The trail's free,
anyhow. If anybody tries to stop us usin' that,
they want to come at us with their guns ready.
Many thanks for your kindness, Mr. Kline!"

"Are you trying to be sarcastic?" Kline asked,
belligerently.

"What do you think?" Riley countered.

He backed out through the door and put on
his hat. Untying his horse, he got into the saddle, taking his sweet time about it. He had a
glimpse of Kline's face at the window as he
swung his horse around and started toward the
lane.

A sweet bunch of mystery around this outfit,
Dan Riley told himself. Hiring outlaws for
assistant foremen, and the girl hinting at trouble, and a superintendent acting in a manner
almost inhuman!

But the only thing that worried him was the
long trip back to Mesaville, and Esteban with

an injured horse. Riley came to the lane and turned down it toward the distant gate. He saw Esteban coming with a couple of the Granton cowboys, and spurred to meet him.

"Want to see you, Esteban," Riley said, having saluted the others.

They rode on, and Esteban stopped.

"How's your horse?"

"He must have tripped, señor, and sprained his leg," Esteban said. "A little rest, and he will be as well as ever. In a pasture, or even a corral where there are not too many other horses—"

"Think he can stand the trip back to Mesaville?"

"Back to Mesaville?" Esteban gasped. "But I thought we had come out here to work. Have you a new insane idea now, Señor Dan? Is it not enough for one day that we ride and fight and get thrown, always with a vision of greasy pots and pans before the eyes?"

"Yeah? You can damned well get that vision out of your eyes," Riley told him. "Even before we start work, we're fired."

"You mean they don't want us?"

"I sure got that impression," Riley said. "No explanations. There's a fancy kind of foreman named Kline, and he says that Mr. Granton changed his mind about wantin' us to work. I asked him to change horses for you, and he wouldn't. On top of that, he didn't want to let us go to the cook shack and eat."

"Señor!" Don Esteban cried. "I never have heard of such a thing. In this country, the wanderer is always welcome to food. I wish you had not mentioned it, Señor Dan. Because of the excitement, I ate little yesterday and last night. This morning I had only a dozen or so tortillas at the hut of my friend. I am famished at this moment."

"Take a tuck in your belt, Esteban," Riley advised. "You won't get any eats this side of Mesaville, far as I know. It's the horse I'm worryin' about."

"He can make the journey, Señor Dan, but it will have to be a slow one."

"That'll be nice, with the sun blazin' down as it is. Can't be helped, I reckon."

"It is Fate!" Don Esteban pronounced.

"We might as well start. I've got a lot of thinkin' to do," Riley told him. "Can't understand this deal. The girl seemed to know that we were comin' to work here—said she might want to see me later and ask me somethin'."

"It will be a terrible ride, but Mesaville will be at the end of it," Esteban said. "The cantina of Pablo Lopez, and his charming dau—I beg pardon, Señor Dan! I almost mentioned a woman."

"I'll stick to my original plan," Riley said. "The men I'm after are comin' to this neighborhood, so I'll just wait for 'em to show up. We've just had a long ride for nothin'."

"And a fight, señor!"

"And a—" Riley stopped speaking, and a peculiar expression came into his face. "Uh-huh! We've got to go back the same way we came. Through that little pass. Now, I wonder—"

"You anticipate another fight, señor? *Dios!*"

"Let's start!" Riley said.

They went through the gate and started along the dusty road beneath the blistering sun, their hats pulled down to shield their eyes, and their neckcloths pulled up so high that they almost met the hats.

They could not travel faster than a walk. Don Esteban's horse limped badly, and should not have been ridden at all. The fine dust swirled around them on the hot wind, and the relentless sun burned them.

Riley was trying to analyze the situation—

and the man Kline. He was commencing to gather some vague ideas regarding the situation. But he told himself that his principal interest in life was to sear the remaining three names off his leather hat band, and that he should think of nothing else.

Bancord! Whalen! Lachmer!

Bully Bancord was all that his name implied, a devotee of all iniquities. He was about fifty, and at least forty of those years had been spent in criminal pursuits. As a boy, he had helped rustle cattle, and at seventeen had slain his first man.

Hank Whalen was tall and thin and noted for his cruelty. He was cold-blooded and steel-nerved, the type to blast a path through life with a six-gun.

And "Dude" Lachmer! There was a rogue! About twenty-eight, tall and handsome, given to fine raiment and fancy boots. But, at his age, he had as many crimes chalked up against him as the others. And he was the worst type— in the game for the excitement as well as the gain.

Riley glanced at Esteban, who had slouched to one side of the saddle and appeared about half asleep. At the rate they were traveling, it would take the remainder of the day to get to Mesaville—if they got there at all.

For Riley was a little apprehensive about this return journey. If Pete Drake and his friends were waiting in ambush again, they might be successful. Esteban's horse could not carry him at any rate of speed.

As they rode along, Riley got his six-gun out of the holster and examined it, made sure that it was loaded. Esteban saw him, and did the same. Their glances met. Presently, they came to a place where rocks flanked a curve and cast some shade, and where there was protection from wind, dust and sun.

There they stopped and dropped their neck-cloths, took swigs of warm water from their canteens, made cigarettes and lighted them, and relaxed for a moment. The horses needed a breathing spell, too.

Riley got down and examined Esteban's horse. It was a bad sprain, he decided, and it would be criminal to make the animal travel fast for even a short distance. His own mount could carry double, but not all the way to Mesaville, and certainly not if they were trying to race with enemies.

"Señor Dan, you seem troubled," Esteban said.

"Don't like the looks of things. You ain't got any business runnin' around with me, Esteban. There you were, a happy cuss wanderin' around and visitin', and singin' for your meals and drink, and never in any trouble. Then you hook up with me. It ain't you these hombres are after. Stay away from me, and you'll stay away from a mess of grief."

"Grief is pleasure when shared with a friend, señor."

Riley grinned. "All right, hombre! Stick! We'll battle our way through no matter what happens."

"Somebody," Esteban observed suddenly, "is coming in a hurry!"

Riley jerked his head around so that his ears caught the wind at the right angle. He heard the pounding of galloping hooves. He jerked out his six-gun, and Esteban did the same, and they backed their mounts off the trail and beneath an overhanging rock.

The hoofbeats came nearer, and nearer. A puff of dust in the distance told where the rider was traveling. The rock-bordered curve hid everything else.

CHAPTER XIII

ANOTHER WAY HOME

AROUND the curve dashed the big black, with Betty Granton in the saddle. She was upon them, past them in a flash, then was fighting to bring the horse under control and stop him, for he had been running free.

She disappeared in a cloud of dust, but, just as Riley and Esteban were preparing to take after her, they saw her coming back. So they waited in the shade beneath the ledge.

"Oh, I'm so glad I overtook you!" she cried.

Her face showed that she recently had indulged in a fit of anger, and that she was not quite over it yet.

"Any trouble?" Riley asked. "You sure were goin'. That black is a great horse."

"And where were you and your friend, Esteban, going?" she asked.

"Back to Mesaville, I reckon."

"Why? I thought you were going to work for Dad."

"So did we," Riley told her. "I reported to that Mr. Kline."

"And what was it he said that made you mad, so you wouldn't take the job?"

"What's that?" Riley cried.

"Kline told Dad that you got mad about something, and wouldn't take the job. Said you seemed to think you'd ought to live at the ranch house and eat with the family, and not do any work."

"Yeah? Some day, somewhere, I aim to meet up with Mr. Kline," Riley declared.

"Just as I thought! He lied when he told Dad all that stuff, didn't he?"

"He sure and certain did. I reported, like I said, and he said your Dad had changed his mind, and that there wasn't any work for Esteban and me. I knew they were hirin' good men wherever they could find 'em, bein' short-handed, so I figured maybe me and Esteban ain't good men."

"What else happened?" Betty demanded.

"Nothin' else could. He said there wasn't any jobs for us, and that settled it, him bein' the foreman. Then I asked could Esteban trade horses, account his bein' hurt, and he said they didn't let everybody have their horses."

"Oh, the beast! And that poor horse scarcely able to walk!"

"Ah, but, beautiful señorita, that is not the worst!" Esteban put in. "The long trip, the excitement—we were famished."

"You mean you were," Riley said.

"And Señor Dan suggested, so he says, that we be allowed to go to the cook shack, and get a little snack of food, and this Señor Kline, he—"

"Refused?" she snapped.

"I reckon," Riley replied.

"Why, that—if it ever gets out it'll disgrace the outfit forever!" she cried. "The beast! The brute!"

"Please, Miss Granton, what happened?" Riley wanted to know.

"I don't know myself. I found that you'd started back, and Kline told Dad that you got mad and wouldn't take the jobs. So I rode after you, to give you a piece of my mind. I'd hinted to you about some things, Riley—"

"The name's Dan."

"All right, Dan. And I thought it was funny you'd go away like that, without saying a word to me. I—I was hoping that you'd help me."

"I'll help you any time I can, sure. What's behind it?" Riley asked.

She glanced toward Esteban.

"Oh, Esteban's all right," said Riley.

"There's some sort of trouble now between Dad and Kline, I think. Kline isn't just an ordinary foreman or superintendent—he represents some of the syndicate's stockholders. So Dad is compelled to listen to him."

"Can't just fire him and kick him out?"

"No." She smiled a bit. "I want you to come back."

"That'd be ridin' right into trouble and fuss," Riley explained. "For some reason, Kline don't want me to work there. It's all right with me. I ain't crazy about takin' a job just now—got somethin' else to do."

"Nor I!" said Esteban. He drew himself up in his saddle. "Because his friend wished it, Don Esteban Marcos Pulido was prepared to wash pots and pans, and even peel potatoes. But his heart will not break if that is denied him, and he be allowed to return to Mesaville and loiter around the cantina."

"I wish you'd come back—Dan."

"Then I'd be the center of trouble, and everybody'd be watchin' me, and I couldn't help you, maybe. Understand?" Riley asked. "Some things you hinted at hook up with some things I know. Maybe I can get better results by hangin' around Mesaville."

"Then I'll keep in touch with you," she said. "If I need you, I'll send one of the boys I can trust with a note. He'll find you if you're in town."

"That'll be fine!" Riley said. "I'll be around somewhere. I've got to keep my eyes on a few hombres."

"The ones we talked about?"

"Yeah!"

"And I'll try to let you know if they come to the ranch without passing through Mesaville first," she said.

Then she touched the black with her tiny spurs, and was away in a cloud of dust, dashing back toward the ranch.

"There goes the sort of señorita," said Esteban, "that love songs are written about."

"Oh, she's all right—for a woman," Riley observed. "You'd better get your mind off that love song mush and put it on somethin' we're liable to run into. It's a long way to Mesaville."

They rode out under the hot sun and followed the winding trail. Mile after mile, with their mounts walking, they endured the heat and the dust. At times, Riley had Esteban get up beside him, and they led the latter's mount.

Then they came to another bunch of rocks, where there was a little shade, and stopped to rest and recuperate. Tobacco and papers came out, after faces had been mopped and swigs taken from the canteens.

"I've been wonderin'," Riley said, as he rolled his cigarette, "whether we might run into some hostile hombres when we come to that little pass."

"Ah, señor! I, too, have been wondering," Esteban replied. "As I told you when first we met, I have a knowledge of this country. Let us not inquire how I got it. I was a young man once, and liked to roam the hills."

"You damned well mean you had to hide out from a posse," Riley told him, "but no matter."

"And it has just occurred to me, señor, that I know a way to Mesaville which does not run through the pass. If enemies are waiting there, we can turn from this trail before they see us."

"That sounds mighty fine, Esteban."

So, when they started out again, Esteban led the way, and they departed from the main trail and went down into a coulee, and from that to a dry watercourse, which they followed on its curving way to the hills.

Since they traveled so slowly, because of Esteban's horse, and the wind was churning the dust from the brush anyhow, there were no lifting puffs of dust to show their progress.

After a long time down there where the sun was hotter and there was not even the warm breeze, they got out of the watercourse and cut across a field of boulders. The pass was behind them, and between them and it was a formation which cut off the view.

Then Esteban led the way into the hills, following a narrow path. Here there was some shade, and grass that was not burned, and finally Esteban called a halt, dropped his neckcloth, waited until Riley had done the same—and smiled.

"Señor Dan," he asked, "how would you like a drink of icy cold water, and to fill your canteen with the same?"

"The heat's gone to your head," Riley said.

"Let us see!"

They dismounted and trailed the reins, and let the horses nibble at the half-green grass. Esteban led the way back through the rocks to a cold spring, where they drank and filled the canteens. The horses could not reach the spring, but they carried water to them in their hats, and also some with which to bathe the leg Esteban's horse had sprained.

"Now we can proceed with some comfort," Esteban said.

"We're goin' a long way around, seems to me."

"There is not the difference of a mile," Esteban assured him. "Around the shoulder of the next hill, we can see Mesaville."

They came to the town an hour and a half later, approaching from the south instead of the north, and put up their horses in Lopez' stable. Esteban attended to the sprain as well as he could.

Then they engaged the same patio rooms they had the night before, and went outside to sit against the wall of the building and smoke and talk, and rest.

It was just before sunset when two horsemen came riding at a leisurely rate of speed down the north trail and toward the cantina. Riley shifted his holster, so the gun would be handy. Esteban took precautions also.

The riders neared the hitch rail, and one of them observed the pair and whispered to the other. The second looked at them, and muttered curses.

"Howdy, Drake!" Dan Riley called. "You look all worn out. Must have been out in the sun all day. Watchin' the pass, maybe, huh?"

CHAPTER XIV

NIGHT came, and the cantina once more became a scene of activity. Men came in off the south trail. Frequently, a heavy vehicle lumbered by. Horses squealed and kicked at the hitch rails.

Dan Riley walked around and listened to the gossip, though pretending not to do so, and Esteban always was near, prepared to give aid if trouble broke out.

Finally, Riley sat in a corner near the piano, while the cantina girls were dancing and sing-, ing, and Esteban, feeling that his friend was safe with his back against a wall, drifted to the bar to talk to a man he knew.

Carmelita Lopez slipped quietly along the wall and stood beside Riley. He got a whiff of perfume, and glanced up at her, to meet a dimpling smile and flashing eyes.

"All dressed up for a killin', huh?" Riley said. "Whose wine are you—"

"Stop, señor! You said that you forgave.

Do not, then, be continually speaking of things."

"You're right, Carmelita. Well, how's everything?"

"Very nice, indeed, Señor Dan. So you did not go to work at the Granton ranch. That is well. You should be above the ordinary punching of cows, Señor Dan. Such a task is beneath you."

"Rats! I punched cows before I joined the Rangers."

"But, since you joined them—ah, no, señor! Too fine a man to be a common cowpuncher. And that Esteban! What a cook he would have made. He rejoices that you did not go to work at the ranch."

"I ain't doubtin' that last statement a bit," Riley told her, laughing.

"Now you are safe, Señor Dan."

"What you mean by that?" he asked.

"You, who hate women so, and would have nothing whatever to do with them—you are safe. Had you worked at the ranch, the yellow-haired girl would have had you. That was her thought, Señor Dan. When you stopped her runaway horse, and rebuked her for not handling him, you won her heart. From that very window, I saw the look in her eyes."

"Yeah? Then the way to win a woman's to rave at her, huh? Just goes to show what sense a woman's got."

She bent forward, as though to slap him on the arm playfully, but in reality so she could whisper: "Order wine, that I may serve it and drink with you. We must talk."

Riley glanced at her swiftly, and caught an expression of seriousness in her face. "Sure!" he said.

She hurried away, her high heels tap-tapping the cantina floor, her head tossed proudly, her skirts swishing from side to side with the swing of her hips. Carmelita was a beauty—and she knew it.

Soon she was back with the wine and glasses on a tray, and sat down beside Riley, and served it. Lopez had a rule in his cantina that no girl could sit at a table with a man unless wine was bought, and even Carmelita observed the rule. The wine also meant that Riley had exclusive right to this girl's company as long as the wine lasted, and nobody would bother them.

"What's troublin' you, if anything?" Riley asked.

"Pretend to be interested, to flirt—smile and laugh," she whispered. "Nobody must dream

that I ever give you information. I overhear a
lot, Señor Dan. But, if they ever suspect me
of telling, they will begin to speak carefully in
my presence, then I never shall learn anything."

"I get it!" Riley said. He laughed a little, as
though at something amusing she had told him.

"Bully Bancord and Hank Whalen passed
through the village of Quebrada this morning,"
she said. "They were riding good horses. They
had packs with them, light ones. They stopped
at Quebrada only for a time at the cantina, and
then took to the trail again."

"Light packs won't slow 'em up. It means
they'll sleep out to-night, maybe in a dry camp,
and come right on. And they'll be here to-
morrow."

"*Sí, señor.* They gave out that they were
coming here to meet Sam Akers, and that—the
expression is Americaño, but I believe I remember it—that they had something soft."

"You've got it, all right," Riley said, and this
time he did not have to pretend to be laughing.
"So Bancord and Whalen are travelin' together.
A couple of hard hombres! Ever hear anything
about 'Dude' Lachmer? You used to like the
Dude, didn't you, Carmelita? He's a handsome
dog."

Her face flamed. *"Si!* He is a dog, Señor Dan! Like him? I detest him. I—"

"That's enough! I just wanted to be sure that you'd tell me the truth where the Dude's concerned, and I reckon you will. Ever hear anything about Lachmer, huh?"

"Only a rumor, señor, that he is to join the others soon. He is at present down in Mexico. They say he is a colonel in the army."

"His own army, maybe," Riley said, laughing again. "Thanks, Carmelita! You're sure a help."

"I am but trying to atone, señor, for the wrong I did you."

"You ain't a bad girl at all," he said.

"You like me a little, Señor Dan?"

"Don't commence that, now!" Riley warned.

"There is something else, too," she said. "It might be wise for you to beware Señor Pete Drake."

"Don't worry. I've got my eyes on him."

"It seems that he and some of his friends have been away all day. One returned with a bullet in his shoulder, and another had been scratched on the wrist. And Señor Drake is very angry about something that did not happen."

"I'm bettin'!" Riley said. "If it'd happened, I wouldn't be here listenin' to you, maybe."

She left him, then, and went back to the piano to sing, and Esteban, who had been waiting and watching in the near distance, hurried up and took the chair Carmelita had vacated.

"Señor Pedro Drake is prowling around like a she-bear who has lost her only cub," Esteban said. "It is in my mind that only one of us sleep at a time, and the other watch."

"Might be a good idea, at that," Riley answered. "You do your sleepin' first."

"But, no, señor! That would not be right."

"You do as I say. You're fat, and need a lot of sleep. Me, I can damned well get along without it. I've slept with one eye open for so long that I never know whether I'm asleep or not."

"As you say, Señor Dan." Esteban yawned.

Half an hour later, they had their nightcap, nodded to Lopez and grinned at Carmelita, and waded through the crowd along the bar to get to the front door. That was Riley's idea, instead of going directly to the patio. He wished to see whether anybody had an undue interest in their movements.

They went out into the moonlight, and walked

down toward the stable, as though to get their horses. In the darkness against the stable wall, they watched.

A man slipped furtively from the shadows and hurried to the cantina, and through a window they could see him say something to Pete Drake. The latter appeared to grow excited. He emerged from the cantina and made his way toward the stable, keeping in the darkness as much as possible. At the side of a clump of brush, he crouched to watch.

"He's sure got a lot of interest in our comin's and goin's," Riley said. "Thinks that maybe we're gettin' our horses to go somewhere. All set to trail us with some of his friends, I reckon."

"*Si!* It will be wise for us to sleep one at a time," Esteban declared.

Drake was growing nervous watching beside the clump of brush. Riley and Esteban went quietly on around the stable, around an adobe hut adjoining it, came to the streak of blackness cast by the cantina building itself, and got inside again. They lounged at the head of the bar and watched the open door.

A moment later, Drake appeared. One of his men undoubtedly had gone out in search of him.

"Howdy, Drake!" Riley greeted. "Been out takin' a walk in the moonlight?"

Drake lurched toward them, his eyes blazing angrily, and Riley quickly balanced his body and bent slightly forward, standing on the balls of his feet, ready for any emergency.

"I'm gettin' pretty sick o' you, Riley!" Drake said.

"Any time you want a pill, Drake, I'll furnish it—a lead one! Does your whole gang run to ambushin'? Better pull in your claws, Drake, and wait for reënforcements. I understand you've got some friends comin' along in a few days."

"If you're wise, Riley, you'll leave Mesaville before they get here."

"I never did have any sense—so I reckon I'll stay."

Drake muttered something and turned away from them, to cross the room. Riley and Esteban went toward the rear of the cantina, where a door opened into the patio.

"Sweet dreams, Esteban," Riley said. "Curl up your fat little tummy, and don't forget to snore."

"I go to my repose this night thankful in particular for one thing," Esteban said. "And it is in my mind to say a prayer for that Señor Kline, who refused me the job of cook's assistant."

Esteban opened the door of the little cell-like room and went inside. Riley remained in the shadows. When he was sure that nobody had seen or heard him, he went to the end of the patio wall, sat upon the ground, and there made himself as comfortable as possible.

If anything happened, it would be at a very late hour, perhaps just before the dawn, when slumbering men sleep soundest, when their brains have toyed with the events of the day before, and run through the gamut of dreams, and finally seek a moment of peace before starting to function again.

For Dan Riley had no intention of arousing Esteban in the middle of the night and letting him stand the second watch. Not that he did not trust Esteban, and not that he doubted his alertness and quick judgment. But Dan Riley liked to attend to his own affairs himself.

Riley had spent a hard day, and the day before had not been of the easiest. But he was at his best when living at high pressure. Rangers lived at high pressure continually—else soon they would cease to live at all.

He slipped into his room and fixed the

blankets on the cot so they would resemble a sleeping man, as he had done the night before. But he did not remain in the room. He estimated that, later, the moonlight, streaming into the room through the little, steel-barred window, would touch that roll of blankets and indicate a human form.

Riley crossed the patio again, keeping in the dark spots, and once more sat down with his back to the wall. He did not smoke, lest the odor or glow of cigarette end betray his presence. Before long, he smiled at the heavy snores that came from the room occupied by Esteban.

There was a din in the cantina, and once he heard a shot, and at another time a girl's angry cry. Horsemen came and went along the dusty trail—those who traveled only at night, and generally knew when it was safe to travel at all.

Riley dozed, awoke, and dozed again. And again he awoke, to find that the moon had wheeled the sky, and that it was about three o'clock in the morning. His hand strayed to his holster, and he drew out his six-gun.

He had seen nothing, but some slight sound had brought him from half-slumber. He did not shift his position, but watched and listened.

And he heard the sound of a boot crunching gravel.

There was a darker shadow against the patio wall, on the opposite side. It moved along the wall slowly, a foot at a time. Without making the slightest noise, Dan Riley got to his feet.

The shadow crept along beneath the arches, from door to door. Finally, it stopped beside the door of Riley's room. Then it slipped along to the window, which was only a hole in the adobe, protected by a network of bars.

In the faint streak of moonlight, Riley could see a man's hand go up, could tell that the hand held a gun. The night was split with flame and shattered with a roar. Three shots barked. Then the man at the window turned and started to run to the end of the patio.

"Here I am, Drake!"

The fleeing man stopped, astounded. In front of him was Dan Riley, standing openly in the moonlight. Drake snarled, and threw up his gun again.

But Dan Riley did not wait for that shot. He placed his own where it pleased him. Drake dropped his gun and reeled back against the patio wall, as the cantina door was hurled open and the big room vomited men into the patio.

"Tried to kill me while I was asleep, huh?".
Riley said. "I put that bullet in your shoulder
on purpose, Drake. It's just a warnin'. Next
time, I'll put it through your heart!"

A score of men had heard the accusation, and
noticed that it had not been denied. Pete Drake,
clutching his wounded shoulder, went through
the gate and out into the night.

"Señor Riley, you are fortunate," Lopez said
to him. "How did you come to suspect the
man?"

Riley grinned in the darkness. "Anybody'd
suspect him, after takin' a good look," he replied.

"There is always trouble wherever you go,
señor."

"He probably ruined one of your best blankets,
Lopez. You better charge it up to him. If he
won't pay, charge it to me. It's been worth it.
Seems to be a nest of ambushers down this Mesaville trail. I yearn to find me a man who'll fight
fair and square out in the open."

They all trooped back into the cantina room,
and, now that the danger was over, Riley made
a cigarette. He puffed in content as he walked
back and forth before going to bed. He stopped

once in front of the little window of the room in which Esteban was sleeping.

Esteban snored. Through it all, he had snored. And, in the morning, he probably would not believe what they told him.

CHAPTER XV

AN UNEXPECTED MEETING

RILEY slept late, which is to say until sunrise. Esteban already was up, and in the cantina, talking to Lopez, who seldom slept at all, fearful that he might miss a few coins if he did.

"Señor Dan!" Esteban cried. "What is this they tell me? Why did you not call to me?"

"You was snorin' somethin' beautiful," Riley said, as he gulped coffee and ate an omelet of peppers and grated chicken.

"It is rumored that Señor Drake had his shoulder mended, got his horse, and set out over the north trail."

"Goin' to meet his friends," Riley said. "A couple of 'em are due from Quebrada to-day. He'll tell 'em that I'm here, and they'll come into town ready to be violent, I reckon."

"More trouble!" said Esteban, and sighed.

"Yeah? I warned you not to tie up with me, Esteban. You'll maybe turn your back on me now. Tell folks you're mad at me and don't like me any more. You may live longer by doin' it."

"It is an insult, that thought!" Esteban cried. "Don Esteban Marco Pulido never deserts a friend. You are the first real one I ever had, Señor Dan, and I cling to you like a cactus spine to a bare foot."

"It's your funeral—maybe," said Riley.

Carmelita came from the kitchen with fresh coffee, and Riley kicked Esteban under the table. "Get away from here," he said. "And you needn't grin like that, either. I ain't makin' love to the girl. She might have somethin' private to tell me about somethin'."

Esteban arose and bowed. "It is not the girl, señor, but the state of mind," he said. "There are other girls—some with golden hair and blue eyes. I shall sing a love song for you yet!"

"You get the hell out o' here!" Riley growled. "I don't like yellow hair any better than I do black."

Esteban departed, and Carmelita approached. Her eyes glistened as she looked at Dan Riley, and she talked as she poured the fresh coffee for him. Nobody was near.

"That was splendid last night, señor," she said. "That Señor Drake—I detest him!"

"You seem to be detestin' almost everybody," he said.

"Not everybody, señor."

"Don't start that, now. What's on your mind this mornin', if anything?"

"I have overheard some things that I do not quite understand, Señor Dan. But I can tell them to you, and perhaps they are worth something, and perhaps nothing."

"What is it?"

"Plans have been made for an enormous number of horses and cattle to be run over the Line."

"They're doin' that every day, Carmelita. Wet cattle. Stolen on one side and sold on the other."

"These are to go from the States to the other side. Thousands and thousands of them, señor, with scores of men in the drive. It is all arranged. It is to happen at a certain time. It is a great plot of some sort, señor."

"Somebody's crazy," Riley declared. "Where the blazes could rustlers get those thousands and thousands, huh? And runnin' them in that direction. Nobody over there to buy that many. Ain't got money enough, even at rustler prices."

"Could they not get the stock from the great Granton ranch, Señor Dan?"

"Sure! That ranch is lousy with stock, horses and cattle both. Owned by a syndicate—five big ranches in one. But it'd be a job, don't you see, Carmelita? Have to be a lot of men in on it. They'd have to make the drive all at once to get away with it, in two nights anyhow. Couldn't be done, unless somebody on the inside—"

Dan Riley ceased speaking, sat up abruptly in his chair as though an electric shock had gone through his body. Somebody on the inside!

"What is the trouble, Señor Dan?" the girl asked.

"Just happened to think of somethin'," he said. "You listen to me, Carmelita. This here might be important—big enough to get the govern- ment interested, even. Learn all you can about it for me, huh?"

"Gladly, señor!" She flushed with pleasure.

"Know any of the men mixed up in it?"

"One of them was talking to Señor Drake."

"I reckon! You prob'ly can expect a lot of strangers around here some night, spendin' their money in the cantina. Then they'll disappear, and you won't ever see 'em again. And a lot of Granton horses and cattle will be disappearin' at about the same time. Now you'd better get away from me. We don't want to be seen talkin' together too much."

"I understand, Señor Dan. Men might think that I was giving you information."

"It ain't that. They might think we was sweetheartin', and that'd be a hell of a lot worse."

Esteban returned, but Riley told him nothing. He wanted to think this thing out. Something big, undoubtedly. And—somebody on the inside! Friction between Granton and Kline, his superintendent, who represented some of the syndicate's shareholders!

Throughout the day, Riley and Esteban rested, and watched the north trail, also the hills to the west. If Drake had gone out to meet Bully Bancord and Hank Whalen, and warn them of Riley's presence, the pair might try to slip into town unobserved and catch Riley off guard.

It was the middle of the afternoon when they saw a puff of dust coming along the trail, a moving black spot ahead of it.

"Somebody in a hurry," Riley said.

"It must be something serious, señor, for him to travel so in the heat of the day. Properly, this is the siesta hour, when a hidalgo does nothing but rest."

"Yeah? You have it your way, you'd be a hidalgo and the siesta twenty-four hours long."

"Don Esteban Marcos Pulido does not believe in useless exertion."

"I can go you one better than that—you don't believe in exertion of any kind," Riley told him, laughing.

They watched the approaching horseman. He was coming at a speed greater than ordinary. The lifting dust cloud trailed behind him like smoke behind a steamship. He swept down the slope and around a curve, disappeared into a depression and emerged, and dashed on toward the town.

"One hombre in a hurry!" Riley commented. "Know him, Esteban?"

"I do not recognize him yet, Señor Dan. But the horse looks like the sort they raise on the Granton ranch."

"Maybe somebody's sick."

"There is no doctor in Mesaville, señor. He died himself, of old age, three years ago."

"Yeah? Maybe it's just some thirsty cowpoke in a hurry to get a drink. Know soon, I reckon."

The horseman cut across the plaza, the hooves of his mount sending the gravel flying. He skidded his horse to a stop and vaulted out of the saddle, trailing the reins and not stopping to tether the horse. Then he hurried into the cantina.

"I said it—in a hurry to get a drink," Riley remarked.

"That is a Granton ranch horse, señor."

"They've got plenty of 'em out there."

"And would not lend one to me. A pest on them!" Esteban pronounced. "I am glad that we did not go to work there, Señor Dan."

"I believe you, Don Esteban!"

Through an open window of the cantina, Lopez thrust his head.

"You out there, Riley?" he howled.

"Right here, Lopez! What's the trouble?"

"Nothing. Just stay there, señor."

Riley and Esteban got to their feet, wondering what that might mean. Out of the cantina door rushed the rider who had just reached the town, to hurry up to them.

"Dan Riley? Got a letter for you," he said, handing it over. "Told me to fan and fog and get it in your hands as soon as possible."

"Wait a minute," Riley said. "You've delivered it, so there ain't any more rush. Light up a cigarette, while I have a look."

As he spoke, he tore open the envelope, and also scrutinized the man who had given it to

him.   He was a young cowpuncher, scarcely
more than a boy.

"Work for Granton?" Riley asked.

"Yeah! That letter's from the ranch."

"So I see," Riley observed.   "I'll be lookin'
into it."

The great Granton ranch had such things as
printed letterheads and envelopes. A glance at
the envelope had confirmed that for Riley. Now
he drew out a folded sheet of paper, and opened
it to find a note written on a printed letterhead.

He read the note swiftly, read it a second time,
while Esteban yawned and pretended not to be
interested, and the messenger did considerable
nervous fidgeting.

There were two notes, strictly speaking. The
first was signed by Bill Kline, the superintendent:

*Mr. Riley:—I made an unfortunate error
yesterday, which I hope you will be broad-
minded enough to overlook. I was laboring
under a misunderstanding.*

*Please come to the ranch at once and
assume the position of assistant foreman Mr.
Granton offered you. You may also bring
your comical friend along.*

The second note was very short, written in a woman's hand. It said: "Please come at once, Dan." And it was signed "Betty."

Riley folded the notes and toyed with them while he looked at the messenger.

"Who gave this letter to you?" he asked.

"Mr. Kline."

"And he told you to find me and deliver it right away?"

"That's right."

"How's things at the ranch?"

"Why, just as usual, I reckon."

"Any men hired to-day—new ones?"

"Not as I know of."

"All right! I'll 'tend to this," Riley said. "Thanks, kid, for gettin' here with it so quick."

"You're the man who shot Sam Akers, ain't you?"

"I am, but I don't like to have such things talked about much."

"I just wanted to say," the boy declared, "that you did a mighty good job."

"A lot of folks agree to that. You'd better rest up yourself and your horse before you go back."

The puncher hurried back into the cantina,

and Don Esteban Marcos Pulido, choking with curiosity, approached his friend.

"A fine lad to be a messenger of love!" said Esteban.   "He rides like the wind—"

"Esteban, brace yourself against the cantina wall," Riley interrupted.   "You're about to be shocked.   We're goin' to do some ridin' our own selves, right away.   That's the first shock.   In this sun and heat, and we're goin' to ride fast. You'll have to borrow a mount from Lopez, so get busy."

"At times friendship is a burden," Esteban observed.

"And here's the second shock, Esteban—we're goin' to work at the Granton ranch after all. They just can't get along without us.   They've sent for us."

"Pots and pans—and potatoes!" said Esteban. "Do you think it wise, Señor Dan?"

"I sure do.   Them hombres ought to be there to-day or to-morrow.   I can handle 'em as well there as here, and maybe better.   You see about that horse."

Esteban went into the cantina, shaking his head as though to say that Fate dealt him many a hard blow.   Riley walked along the hitch rail and inspected the horse of the messenger.   He watched the nostrils, the heaving sides, felt of the wet skin, inspected the mouth foam, and the lather at the edge of the saddle blanket. Then he grinned.

"Rode like hell to get here," he muttered. "He rode like hell from the top of that hill three miles away, knowin' he could be seen—but he was doin' ordinary ridin' before that."

Then he hurried to the stable to get his own horse ready, and Esteban appeared with Lopez to get ready another horse. They led the mounts out and across to the cantina hitch rail.

"Lopez, I want to borrow a couple of rifles and some ammunition," Riley said. "One for me and one for Esteban. I know you've got plenty of guns."

"Rifles, señor?" Lopez gasped. "You are going hunting, perhaps?"

"Yeah! And maybe after big game." . . .

Through the sun they rode, taking the messenger along with them. He had a fresh horse, for the Granton ranch always kept a couple in Lopez' stable for the use of their men.

When they came to the broken country, Riley got his rifle handy, and Esteban, as usual, emulated him. The cowpuncher seemed surprised.

"Lookin' for trouble?" he asked.

"We had some yesterday," Riley told him. "We're ready for it to-day."

"What's all the fuss about, anyhow?" the boy asked. "I know about you, of course, and how you've been lookin' for some men, and how you got Sam Akers, and about your hat band—"

"Better stop, or you'll choke," Riley advised. "There's nothin' to it, boy, except this—some gents are out to get me, and I'm out to get them, and both of us want to be the first to do the gettin'. It's simple."

"Yeah, I see it is."

" 'Bout as simple as you are. I had a look at your horse. He'd been lathered for three or four miles, and no more. You didn't ride like hell all the way from the ranch."

The boy looked alarmed. "Don't you tell the boss," he begged. "It was so hot, and I didn't see any sense in hurryin' so much. But, when I got in sight of the town—"

"Uh-huh! It'll be hotter, for you, if there's any crooked work along this trail, such as ambushin'."

But there was no ambush, much to Riley's surprise and Esteban's delight. They got safely through the pass and into the open, and headed for the ranch, the buildings of which they could see in the distance.

Dan Riley began to feel ashamed that he had suspected anything wrong. Perhaps Betty Granton merely had got her father and Kline together on the subject of hiring him. She wanted him there, feeling that she could trust him.

And Riley wanted to be there, because the three men he sought would be there soon, and because he wanted to solve the mystery that seemed to hang around the big ranch.

They came to the end of the lane. Riley scrutinized everything within sight. Everything seemed to be normal. A few men were working down by the barns and horse corral, and a couple were sitting on a bench in front of the bunk house.

"Reckon we'd better ride down to Kline's office, to find what all this is about," Riley said.

He led the way, Esteban close behind him, the horses at a walk. The young puncher turned and made for the horse corral, to put up his mount. Riley dismounted in front of the little office building and tied his horse, and Esteban remained in the saddle.

"Señor Dan, I shall not get on the ground until I am sure we are to remain," Esteban said. "The people around this ranch have the habit of changing their minds. No doubt, we shall be sent away again."

Riley laughed and knocked on the door.

"Come in!" He recognized the gruff voice of Bill Kline.

Riley opened the door and stepped inside, hat in hand. He regretted that fact an instant later. Even dropping a hat takes a fraction of a second, and that length of time often is important in drawing a gun.

On either side of the door, a man was standing. From either side, Dan Riley felt the muzzle of a gun jab him suddenly in the ribs.

"Get 'em up!" one of the men growled.

The other knocked Riley's hand aside and got the six-gun out of his holster.

"What's all this?" Riley demanded. "You sent for me, didn't you, Kline?"

"I did, yes. I wrote that letter."

"Then why have a couple of hombres stick me up?"

"Just wanted to get your gun away, Riley. You boys can clear out now."

The gun muzzles were removed, the two men went out and closed the door. Riley saw that Bill Kline had a gun on his desk before him.

"You needn't be afraid of me, Kline," Riley said. "I ain't killin' mad over what happened yesterday."

"Nobody's afraid of you, Riley. . . . Come out, boys!"

From behind the big filing cases in a corner, two men stepped forth—Bully Bancord and Hank Whalen.

CHAPTER XVI

DON ESTEBAN SINGS

DON ESTEBAN MARCOS PULIDO, slouching in his saddle with the natural grace of fatigue, surveyed this great ranch upon which he found himself, and decided that there were many men working here, which meant considerable grub and many, many pots and pans—and potatoes.

He tried to tell himself, did Don Esteban, that his was not to be menial labor. True, he would appear as assistant to a cook, but in reality he was a secret agent in disguise, helping his superior unearth a plot and bring terror to evildoers.

That made him feel better, and Don Esteban looked down toward the corrals where some of the fine Granton horses were kept, and toward the calf pasture where every calf was supposed to be worth a small fortune. He glanced at the huge barns filled with feed and implements and tools. The bunk houses—there were two—were such as Don Esteban never had seen before.

Newly constructed, they were of adobe on a steel frame, very sanitary, with good ventilation and all that.

That made the place more a factory than a ranch, Don Esteban thought. Where was the romance? Yet he could imagine himself sitting on a bench near the bunk house door, on a moonlight night, playing a guitar and singing softly, while the punchers gathered around to listen.

He saw the door of the office open, and two men come out. Esteban gave them a single glance and decided that they were two ordinary cowpokes who had been in to see the foreman, probably to get hired or fired. That was all cowboys did—get hired, fired, drunk and broke.

They sauntered toward Esteban, but seemingly gave him no attention. With his forearms folded across the pommel of his saddle, and his eyes half closed, Esteban bent forward, comfortably relaxed, and looked over their heads.

"Look at this, hombre!" one of them said to him, stopping beside the horse.

Esteban looked, then sat erect. What he saw was the muzzle of a gun pointing at his head.

"Step right down out of that saddle and tie your horse," the other commanded.

Resistance would have been futile, and Esteban knew it. He stepped down, and he tied the horse. Then, with a man on either side of him, he was conducted down toward one of the barns.

"What is the meaning of this, señores?" Esteban asked. "Is it possible that you make a mistake?"

"No mistake, hombre! We've got orders to put you in a safe place."

"What has become of Señor Riley?"

"He's in the office. Step along!"

One prodded him with a gun muzzle, and Esteban stepped along.

They took him to a long, low adobe building, opened a door and shoved him in, closed the door and put up the heavy bar which secured it.

Esteban blinked to focus his eyes. He found that he was in a big tool shed, in which at present there were scarcely any tools. He got to a window, which was only about a foot square and would not have admitted of the passage of his body, even if steel bars had not been over it.

Through that window, he had a noble view of countless acreage and a background of hills dotted with thousands of beef critters and horses. But Esteban did not care to look at cattle and horses, or hills.   He wanted to know what was going on.

The secret agent, it appeared, had met with disaster, even before he got to his pots and pans. . . .

Back in the office building, Dan Riley had stood against the wall to look at the men before him.   There was Bully Bancord, his swarthy face asnarl, and Hank Whalen looking at him from beady eyes.   Killers, both.

"Walked right into it," Bully Bancord said.

"Got him!" Hank Whalen added.

"I imagine it was the lady's note that brought him," Kline put in, laughing a bit.   "Anyhow, he's here."

"You've been raisin' hell, ain't you, Riley?" Bancord said.   "Plugged Bill Morgan, and shot up Sam Akers, then nicked Drake in the shoulder.   Must think you're an army."

"Been all over the country lookin' for us, huh?" Whalen asked.   "Well, you've found us."

Dan Riley spoke for the first time since their appearance from behind the cabinets: "That's the same thing Sam Akers said."

"Yeah?" Bancord snarled.   "You won't handle us like you did Akers."

"When are you goin' to kill me?" Riley asked.
"Goin' to wait till night, so there won't be too
many get wise? Think the two of you can do it,
me without a gun? Maybe you'd better call in a
few more of your gang. Kline, there! He
looks like a killer—if the other man's back was
turned."

"Damn you, Riley!" Kline roared. "I won't
stand too much, no matter what—"

He stopped when Bancord gave him a swift
look.

"Thanks!" Riley said. "You tipped off just
what I wanted to know. You've got some reason
for wantin' to keep me alive for awhile. Glad
of that! Maybe you want Dude Lachmer to be
here for the big party. That'd make it com-
plete."

"Talkin' big, ain't you?" Whalen asked.

"Talkin' the way a decent man, and an officer
of the law, ought to talk to outlaw scum!"

"You're pilin' up agony for yourself," Bancord warned.

"What are you goin' to do with me?" Riley
asked. "Let's have it."

"No sense in tellin' you now. We'll let you
think about it and do some guessin'." It was
Whalen who replied.

"Tie his wrists behind his back and take him away," Kline ordered, suddenly, in a voice of authority. "And treat him right. He's a good man, at that. Stick to the program, boys."

Whalen and Bancord advanced upon him, and Riley knew it would be useless to attempt a fight. Either of these men was as strong as he, and there was also Kline to be taken into consideration. If he fought, they would simply crack him on the head with a gun barrel, and then tie his wrists. And he wanted a clear head.

They lashed his wrists, opened the door, and led him out. Down toward the adobe tool shed they took him, in the wake of Esteban and his escort. They opened a door, thrust him inside, and closed the door again.

"Try to get out of that," Whalen barked at him, after the door was closed. "We'll be down to see you later, Riley."

Then they went away.

The tool shed was a long building of two rooms. They had put Esteban in one, and Riley in the other. It took Riley only a few seconds to convince himself that getting out of the shed was practically an impossibility.

"Señor Dan!"

Riley barely could hear the voice. He hurried to the wall between the two rooms.
"Yeah?" he asked.

"This is Esteban. What has happened, señor?"

"Bancord and Whalen are here. They caught me neat. Kline, the foreman, is in with them. I don't know what's goin' on."

"And what shall we do now, señor?" Esteban asked. "We must escape. It is unthinkable that Don Esteban Marcos Pulido should be incarcerated in such a vile place, with dust and cobwebs, and perhaps rats and vermin."

"How's it look on your side?"

"Like a fortress," said Esteban. "It would take dynamite to make a way out."

"Keep lookin' around, and I'll do the same over here. We may find somethin'."

As he searched around the room in which they had imprisoned him, Dan Riley was doing some heavy thinking. He did not believe that Betty Granton had written that note as a decoy. No doubt, she had been hold by Kline that he was sincere in bringing Riley out to work. Probably she had not known that Bancord and Whalen had reached the ranch.

Riley guessed that Drake had gone out to meet them, had told them what had happened, and they had turned from the trail and gone to the ranch instead of continuing on to Mesaville.

What was behind the whole thing, Riley could only guess. And that was something to be considered in the future. The first thing was to get out of this predicament.

He searched around the room in which he found himself, trying to find a way out. There was but the one door, and two windows. The windows were impossible as avenues of escape. The door was heavy and thick, with the hinges embedded in the adobe, and was fastened on the outside with a heavy metal bar. That, too, seemed impossible.

He held speech with Esteban again, and the latter reported no success.

"It will be a terrible place, señor, in which to spend the night," Esteban said. "Ah, if we had remained at the Mesaville cantina! Think, señor. Even now we could be eating and drinking, and that so charming Carmelita would be flirting with you."

"Shut up!" Riley barked at him.

"It comes to me, señor, that now I have you at

a disadvantage. You cannot get out, nor get at me, no more than I can at you. If I were to sing a love song now, even without the guitar—"

"You do, and I'll murder you!"

"But you cannot reach me, señor. And I feel a song coming on. Whenever I am sad, a song comes on to lighten my heart. And it makes me sad to be thus incarcerated, like some common felon."

"Oh, yeah? You had your deserts, you'd be doin' time," Riley told him.

"I wonder whether we shall have food. From this window I can smell delicious odors coming from the cook shack."

They had food. A moment later, men came to the tool shed, armed men who made sure that the prisoners would not escape. They opened the door and thrust a basket in at Riley, and did the same for Esteban, also a bottle of water for each.

Riley did not know these men.

"What's the program?" he asked.

"We ain't talkin'," one of them replied. "You'll prob'ly find out to-morrow."

Then they went away. To-morrow! That meant they were to be left in the tool shed all night. An entire night in which to work their way to liberty—but a task which seemed impossible. No doubt, there would be guards.

They ate, each saving some of the food for later, and drank sparingly of the water. The darkness deepened. Night came down from the hills, and the moon came up.

"Señor Dan!"

"Yeah?" Riley asked.

"Regarding that love song, señor—I feel that I must sing it. I can sing it in Spanish."

"But I understand Spanish, damn it!"

"It is quite true that love is the same in any language."

"You're an ass!" Riley exploded.

"It is also true, señor, that in the north corner of the dividing wall there is a flaw. It originally was a flaw in construction, and the adobe has crumbled, and the rats I but now despised have enlarged it. Have you tools on your side?"

"Sure!" Riley betrayed a little excitement.

"Suppose, señor, that you take a pick and get to work enlarging the hole. We can be together, at least. Together, we may do more than when separated. I know a trick."

"That's great, Esteban!"

"You do the digging, señor, and I shall sing to cover the noise you make, if any guard is outside the shed. Also, from this window I can see if one approaches."

"Start your singin'," Riley told him.

CHAPTER XVII

INTO THE OPEN

DON ESTEBAN MARCOS PULIDO lifted his voice in song. He stood at the open window. His was not a bad voice, at that. And he seemed to put heart into his singing.

Riley got the pick, found the flaw in the wall, and began his work. It was difficult in the dark, but he kept at it. Half his blows went where he did not wish them to go. However, after a time he could tell that the hole was getting larger.

He had some matches, and he risked lighting one and making a better and closer examination of the excavation. After that, he worked to better advantage.

Esteban ceased his song, and Riley his labor while both rested. They got down close to the earth and talked through the hole.

"Señor Dan!"

"Yeah?"

"I am quite sure that my song is appreciated."

"The hell it is! I'm endurin' it only 'cause it covers the noise I'm makin'."

"But certainly such a fine song could not be appreciated by a man without soul, such as yourself, my friend. I was not referring to you."

"What do you mean, Esteban?"

"You were not listening to the words? I sang several verses, as would anybody, and then I used words of my own, señor! I said brave men were imprisoned in the shed of tools, and for a light to be shown at the window three times if there was hope of rescue."

"What damned foolishness—"

"And the lamp was shown three times, señor, a moment ago."

"What? Who'd do it? Must have just happened that way."

"Who? The beautiful— But I am not allowed to mention women!"

"Mention it this once and tell me what the blazes you mean."

"The Señorita Betty, no less. Some months ago, when I was in Mesaville, I sang for her at the general store. And this song is the one she liked best—a bit from Old Spain. So I repeated it, and put in the extra verses. I am sure she understood, for the light appeared at the window."

"What can she do, if she did understand?" Riley asked. "There's somethin' goin' on at this ranch that's so big it's got me guessin'. I don't think the girl and her father are in on it. It's a chance they may be watched."

"When you are ready to continue the digging, señor, I'll sing some more."

"Go ahead. I'll have to stand it."

Esteban sang again, a different song this time, and Riley kept busy with the pick. A chunk of adobe fell out. After that, it was easier. Within a quarter of an hour, he squeezed through the hole and stood beside Esteban.

"A lot of work," Riley said. "And what comes of it? We can't get out this end any better than at the other. But we're together."

"That is something, Señor Dan. If we could but decoy some man here to open the door—"

"Wait, and let me think!" Riley said. "That's an idea. They'd be lookin' for only one man in each room, huh? Esteban, here's where we get out, if anybody's watchin' the shed. But gettin' out won't be enough. We've got to get guns, make a break, then come back and do things!"

"How shall we attract attention, señor? To cry out—"

"That might not be enough," Riley said. "They wouldn't pay any attention to us, maybe. Wait!"

He struck a match and looked around the room. Something he saw on the opposite side attracted him. Riley went over, and struck another match.

What he saw was a pile of old sacks that had contained fertilizer—dry old sacks that would burn readily and also send up a huge cloud of smoke. And above them, on a wide shelf, were cans of paints and oils left over from painting one of the big barns.

He explained rapidly to Esteban:

"We'll start it in the other room. The flames and smoke will shoot through the window. That side of the shed is away from the house and bunk house. It'll look like the big barn on fire, and bring everybody."

"Splendid, señor!"

"It'll make it as hot as hell in this room, though. And we'll have to have something ready to plug up that hole, or the smoke'll come in here and kill us off."

Riley got through the hole, and Esteban

passed through the sacks, paints, oils. Then he prepared something with which to stop up the hole, while Riley, in the other room, arranged the sacks under the window, drenched them with oil, heaped cans of paint upon them.

"Get ready in there, Esteban!" he called.

"I am ready, señor."

Riley touched it off, got to the hole and through it, and stretched out on the floor to watch. The tiny flame caught and spread. The sacking began to burn. A cloud of smoke was pulled through the window by the wind, and flames shot out after it.

They blocked up the hole, and rushed to a window to watch. Both Riley and Esteban began yelling. Men rushed out of the bunk house, and out of the ranch house. The ranch bell began ringing.

Down toward the tool shed rushed a score of men. Hank Whalen was with them, though Bancord was not. But others in the group knew of the prisoners in the tool shed.

"Get 'em out!" Whalen cried. "They'll roast in there!"

Esteban was at the window, begging for release.

"The smoke, señors! It stifles! Poor Señor Riley—in the other room—"

They did not have any particular fear of Esteban, so Whalen told a couple of the men to get him out. They thought that Riley was in the other room. Riley stood beside the door as it was opened, and Esteban was in front of it, back a short distance, and reeling as though about to fall. They had pulled out the stuffing in the hole, and smoke was pouring into the room.

The door was opened, and those outside saw Esteban as though about to fall, overcome by the smoke. Two men remained to attend to him, and the others rushed to the other end.

That was what Riley had been hoping for. One of the men rushed in and caught Esteban as he was about to fall. But Esteban suddenly regained strength, it seemed, and began fighting. The other man started in to aid his comrade.

Riley struck him with the handle of the pick, and he went down. He ran forward, and struck the one wrestling with Esteban. Both men were ranch night guards, and wore guns.

Riley and Esteban got the guns.

"At my heels!" Riley snapped.

"On them, señor, if you do not step lively enough."

They rushed through the smoke and turned toward the dark side of the building. There they stopped an instant, getting the smoke out of their smarting eyes. Then they started on, making for the dark spots.

They came to a tiny gulch, dropped into it, panting. Back at the tool shed was a chorus of yells, and they could hear Hank Whalen howling for Kline. The escape had been discovered.

"Where do we go now, señor?" Esteban asked.

"I thought maybe you'd like to sing a song."

"Music is not in me at the moment, señor. My effort was for nothing. I asked a señorita to save us—then we save ourselves."

"She knows we're around here somewhere, and she may need our help," Riley said. "The main thing now is to get away and hide. I want 'em to think we've made a run for it. So, we'll get down to the horse corral."

Riley started off, Esteban keeping as close to him as possible. They kept to the shadows, and moved by a circuitous route. Men were scattering away from the tool shed and barn in every direction, commencing the search for them.

Others came hurrying from the bunk house, carrying lanterns. The sacking had burned, and the flames had died down. The heavy pall of smoke drifted low over the ground.

They circled the big barn and one of the bunk houses, and came to the horse corral. There should have been a guard at the corral, but he had gone to the fire.

"Get the gate open," Riley whispered. "Then get out of the way. I'll go on the other side and start somethin'."

Esteban opened the big corral gate. Riley went around to the opposite side and got upon the fence. The horses in the corral—some twenty of them—already were excited because of the fire and confusion. Dan Riley gave a yell that started them. They began rushing around the corral. One found the gate open, and dashed out. Others followed.

Past the bunk house the frenzied animals tore, some to run on past the barn and toward the pasture, others to turn toward the lane and thunder down it toward the distant road.

"They're gettin' away!" somebody shouted. Riley thought he recognized Kline's voice. "Saddle up and take after 'em! Plenty of horses in the other corral!"

Riley and Esteban slipped back into the shadows, retreated for a hundred yards, and finally stopped at the edge of a gulch where there were large rocks behind which they could hide.

They were free, they each had a gun, and it was thought they had ridden for the trail, so the pursuit would go there.

"Not bad at all," Riley said. "But we've got work to do when things quiet down."

CHAPTER XVIII

A PLOT OVERHEARD

HALF the men saddled up and took after the fugitives, as they supposed. They dashed for the road, went in all directions, the majority starting a race for town, thinking that Riley and Esteban had gone that way, realizing that if they had not here was a chance to visit the cantina for a couple of hours and have a good excuse for doing so.

Those who remained at the ranch went to the bunk houses to turn in for the night. There was a light in the office building, and the ranch house was ablaze with light on the lower floor. The night guards had resumed their stations.

Riley and Esteban watched the scene from a distance, ready to drop into the gully and get away if anybody approached.

"Our horses have run away with the others, Señor Dan," Esteban said.

"We don't need horses now. We ain't goin' anywhere."

"You mean to remain here, señor?"

"Two of the men I want are here."

"But they have so many friends here, also," Esteban protested.

"And some decent folks might be in trouble, and need our help. We'll wait a little longer, and investigate."

"It is good to stretch out on the cool earth and watch the moon."

"You mean you're takin' a night siesta," Riley told him.

"Señor Dan, you are one of these men who must be always dashing about over the earth. I am one who seeks repose and exists with the least possible effort. Your method gets you trouble, and mine gets me peace."

"You didn't have to pal up with me. I told you—"

"Friendship comes only at a price, Señor Dan. I am making no complaint. But let me sing a song now and then, and I'll gladly join in the fighting."

"Yeah, and there may be some, at that," Riley said. "We've got off pretty easy so far."

"How is that, señor?" Esteban sat up quickly. "We have got off easy so far, you say. *Dios!* In the town and on the trail, and here at the ranch—always a fight! We shoot men, and they shoot at us. They try to murder us in our beds. They waylay us on the trail. They put us in tool sheds and we start a fire and a horse stampede. It is nothing, I suppose—nothing!"

"Practically nothin'," Riley said.

"And when may I expect to see something, señor—tell me that? I should like a bit of excitement now and then. It adds spice to life. I do not wish to grow stale."

"You stick around with me, Esteban, and you won't get old enough to grow stale."

"I believe you, señor," Esteban said, and sighed. "What do we do next?"

"We're goin' to do some prowlin' around the big house, and we sure want to be careful that no guard sees us. On your toes, Esteban!"

Esteban groaned, and got up. But Riley knew the attitude was assumed. Esteban was not fooling him at all. Riley knew that he was alert, cautious, courageous, and loyal.

They slipped through the shadows and reached the lane, where the overhanging trees made an avenue of darkness. Along this they went, walking on the grass. As they neared the house, Riley signaled a stop.

Crouching against the bole of a big tree, they watched and listened for a time. There was no guard at the house, evidently. So Riley led the way forward again.

They came to the corner of the veranda, and followed the side wall. A lighted window was ahead of them—a window which was raised at the bottom a few inches. Riley made for it.

He could hear voices. Pressing close against the wall, he edged forward and risked peering into the room beneath the shade.

John Granton was sitting at one end of a long table. Kline was walking around, doing the talking. Bully Bancord and Hank Whalen were in the room also.

"Understand me, Granton, if you don't come in with us, we'll keep you prisoner here in your own house till it's over," Kline was saying.

"I'll make no deal with a bunch of crooks, Kline," Granton said.

"We'll make you look like a crook, too, so you might as well get some of the profit."

"You haven't explained the scheme to me entirely."

"That isn't necessary. You don't have to know everything. It's enough for you to know that a lot of stock is going to be missing. You won't be able to account for it. You'll report that everything is being done, with no results.

Kick to the government about it, and let 'em call out the fool cavalry, if they want to—when it's too late to do anything."

"You're running the stock into Mexico, naturally," Granton said. "You'd not dare do anything else. But, what can you do with it over there?"

"That's our business."

"I can't believe it of you, Kline. You represent thirty per cent of the shareholders of the syndicate. You're robbing them."

"I represent 'em, and get damned little out of it. My shares aren't big enough to turn me in great profits."

"And these men associated with you!" Granton exclaimed. "They're criminals!"

"Plenty good enough," Kline told him. "Preachers couldn't do the job. These men know the country. They've lived over the Line."

"What is it you wish me to do, Kline?"

"Make fake reports to the company's headquarters and the big shareholders. Cover us."

"Which means that you'll raid again and again, steal more stock."

"Right. Work over the brands, too. But that won't bother us much. This stock is goin' to stop finally up in the hills where there aren't many questions asked."

"I'll have nothing to do with it, Kline."

"It's your say, Granton. Then we'll keep you prisoner till we're in the clear. You'll be sick in bed, if anybody comes callin'. And your girl —we'll keep Betty in her rooms on the upper floor. She won't get a chance to tip off anything. I can handle the situation. Our men are watching the others. If there's trouble, our men will 'tend to 'em, and have a story to tell if the sheriff comes fussing around."

"Kline, you're a scoundrel!" Granton cried. "You'll never get away with this!"

"That's enough! Get to your bedroom, and' go to bed. Stay there, too. You'll be fed at regular hours. And there'll be a guard outside your door, and one outside the window."

"If you harm Betty, or even offer her an affront—"

"Nobody'll harm your girl, but she's going to be kept a prisoner. I'll let you two see each other now and then."

"How long must we be kept this way?" Granton asked.

"Three or four days. We aren't quite ready

to move the stock yet. I have more men coming
—men we can trust. Come on, Granton—get to
bed! Bancord, you and Whalen go to the office
building and wait for me there. We've got to
have a talk to-night."

"Don't forget that we want Dan Riley's hide,"
Bancord said. "He's just fool enough to stumble into the middle of the plot, and spoil things."

"The men'll get him, even if they have to
follow him to Mesaville. I'll be along as soon
as I've posted the guards."

Dan Riley slipped back into the shadows with
Esteban, and they circled the house and went
toward the office building. Riley was doing
some heavy thinking again.

"Ropes, Esteban!" he said, presently.

"Ropes, señor?"

"Three or four of 'em, Esteban. Saddles
stacked down by the corral. Watch out for the
guards. Get the ropes and bring 'em to me,
huh? I'll be at the side of the office buildin'.
And make it quick!"

"You have another idea, señor?"

"Plenty of 'em."

"And will this one 'tend toward excitement,
Señor Dan?"

"This one will be real excitement itself, Esteban. This will be the real thing. Ropes! Then, four horses, with saddles and bridles on 'em."

"You are ordering an army," Esteban complained. "Who am I but a worm? I obey, señor!"

Esteban slipped into a dark patch and disappeared. Riley went on toward the office, moving cautiously, alert for the guards.

Near the office, he crouched in the darkness and waited. Bully Bancord and Hank Whalen came down from the house together, and went into the office. Riley crept nearer.

It was some time later when Kline appeared, striding through the moonlight. He entered the office and closed the door. Riley crept up beside the building and listened beneath a window.

They were talking openly now about their plans, and Riley got enough to understand. His eyes opened wide when he comprehended the scheme. He had heard of rustlers before, but never of anybody stealing practically the entire stock of a huge ranch.

Kline and some others had a vast acreage of leased land in the Mexican hills. They would

run over the stock and hold it on their range.
Thousands and thousands of the finest horses
and cattle. Stock ready to be marketed, stock
for breeding purposes. They would leave on
the Granton ranch only a few scattered animals
that would not make even a decent herd at
roundup time.

Riley smiled as he listened. Did Kline think
that he could manage the rogues with whom he
dealt? They would aid him now. But, once
the stock was over the Line and on the new
range, Mr. Kline would find them turning
against him, kicking him out under some subter-
fuge, possibly even killing him to get him out of
the way.

A sibilant hiss attracted Riley's attention. Esteban was at hand. Riley slipped back through
the shadows to his side.

"Señor, I have here four good ropes," Esteban
said. "Some of the horses have returned to the
corral. There are plenty of saddles and bridles."

"Great!" Riley exclaimed.

"And what is the program now, Señor Dan,
if I may ask?"

"We're goin' to capture a couple of hombres,
Esteban."

"The Señors Bancord and Whalen?"

"That's right!"

"Don Esteban Marcos Pulido—helping catch wildcats! My friends would not believe it."

"I'll let you sing to 'em on the way—just so you don't sing love songs."

"On the way where, señor?"

"You'll be surprised," Riley told him. "The tough job is goin' to be gettin' four horses ready for the trail without bein' caught at it."

"Ah! That reminds me, Señor Dan, my friend! The guard at the horse corral ran across me while I was getting the ropes. I was compelled to hit him twice with the barrel of my gun, and I fear that I cut his head a little. Not wishing to be distressed by his cries of pain, I gagged him with his own neckcloth, then used another rope with which to bind him and tie him to the fence."

"Yeah?" Riley chuckled. "Esteban, you ain't no song singer. You're a tough hombre! That's what kept you so long, huh?"

"And now what, Señor Dan?"

"You stay right here and wait."

Riley went to the window again to listen. He got more details. And presently he rushed back beside Esteban, hissed a warning at him, and crouched behind a rock. The door of the office was opened, and the three men came out.

"See you early in the morning," Kline told the others. *"Buenas noches!"*

CHAPTER XIX

LEAD FLIES AGAIN

KLINE had a room in the ranch house, and there he went. Bancord and Whalen had been assigned a small adobe hut near the barn. They hurried toward it now.

Riley and Esteban trailed them, the latter carrying the ropes and wondering what was about to happen. They crept close to the hut and listened while Bancord and Whalen hurried with their undressing.

"They've turned in, all right," Riley whispered. "Now we've got to get busy, Esteban."

"Get busy, señor? We have been stretched out resting, I suppose. Now we are going to get busy, eh?"

"That's right. We want four horses ready for the trail. If you took care of the corral guard, everything's all right. I've spotted only one other guard around the main buildings, and he's up by the ranch house. But we'll be careful, just the same. Don't forget that there's a moon."

Keeping to the shadows, they came to the

horse corral, and looked over the stock as well as they could. Riley's horse was there, and the one Esteban had ridden out from town. They got saddles and bridles ready, and Riley called softly to his horse.

Letting the animal out the gate, Riley got bridle and saddle on him, and mounted. Then Esteban opened the gate, and Riley rode inside. He roped the horse Esteban had used, and got him out.

It took time to rope two more and prepare them for the trail. But it finally was accomplished, and then Riley and Esteban mounted, and each led another horse, and they rode away from the corral and down into the gulch, to follow it until they were back of the shed where the two men were sleeping.

They tied all the horses to a hitch rail and crept up to the shed. Through the open window, snores rolled out at them. Dan Riley knew there would be no lock on the door.

"We capture 'em, Esteban—understand?" Riley whispered. "And we don't want any noise about it. You got those ropes?"

"They are here by the wall, señor."

"We won't dare light the lantern, but there's moonlight enough in the hut for our work. This is goin' to be a ticklish job, Esteban. Bancord and Whalen ain't babies."

"Would it not be best, señor, to crack them upon their heads first?"

"You're gettin' to be a blood-thirsty wretch, Esteban."

"Evil associations ruin many men," Esteban observed. "I was once calm and peaceful, a lover of music and the poets—but that was before I met you."

They slipped around to the door, and Riley opened it gently. Guns held ready, they crept inside, and closed the door behind them. For a moment they were silent and motionless against the wall.

The two men were sleeping soundly. Riley and Esteban crept carefully up to the cots. Riley pressed Esteban's arm in signal.

Guns were jammed against the heads of two sleeping men. They came awake to a full realization of their position, except that they could not see their captors plainly enough to establish identity. Riley spoke:

"Not a move, hombres, 'less you're ready to die! Roll over on your faces!"

A little persuasion, and they rolled over, and had their wrists bound behind their backs. Then they turned over again, and were gagged effectually with their own neckcloths. After that, they were forced to sit up on their cots.

"We're goin' away from here, hombres," Riley told them. "I ain't got time to let you put on the rest of your clothes—ain't goin' to run the risk. You've both got on full-length underwear, and that's lucky, 'cause you might catch cold otherwise. Step along, gents!"

Their hands were tied behind their backs. Around the neck of each was the noose of a lariat. They were pulled out of the adobe hut and taken behind it, flinching as the gravel bit into the soles of their bare feet.

When they came to the horses, they were compelled to mount, and Riley tied their ankles beneath the horses' bellies. It had been so easy that it seemed ridiculous. Bancord and Whalen had no chance to put up a fight without risking death. And they had recognized Riley, and knew that he would not hesitate to shoot them.

Each had decided to wait for a chance and make a desperate move. They had not expected the horses. And now they were mounted, and their horses were being led by Riley and Esteban, and they were taken into the gulch and along it, traveling until the ranch buildings had been left far behind.

Emerging from the gulch, Riley turned north across country, traveling where there was no trail. When he thought it was safe, he stopped the horses and removed the gags from the two men, and gave them water from a canteen.

"What you think you're doin', Riley?" Bancord demanded. "You know what'll happen to you for this, don't you?"

"You ain't in any position right now to threaten," Riley told him.

"Where are you takin' us?"

"You'll find out that later. Just now, we're makin' for the hills. Want to be in 'em before daylight."

"Our friends'll trail and catch you. Then you won't last five minutes."

"Two seconds before they blast me, you'll be blasted," Riley said. "Let's travel." . . .

Daybreak found them far up in the hills, cutting across to a trail Esteban knew. When they found it, they stopped to give the horses a breathing spell.

"Señor Dan, life grows tame," Esteban said. "We have not been in any fighting for several hours. I thought, when I became your friend, that each day would be filled with tension."

"I know," Riley replied. "It's too damned quiet."

"*Sí, señor!* I feel a song coming on."

"Choke it back," Riley advised. "We ain't advertisin' our whereabouts any."

Bully Bancord barked out a string of profane words. "What are you goin' to do with us?" he cried. "We ain't got on any clothes but our underwear."

"Yeah! That's sure goin' to shock the county-seat, if we get there by daylight."

"Countyseat!" Whalen cried.

"That's where you're goin'—to jail! Bad hombres, huh? Tough gents! Maybe so. But I'm takin' you to jail in your underwear, 'stead of doin' you the honor of shootin' it out with you."

"Damn you, Riley!" Bancord cried. "If you do—"

"You won't do anything about it, 'cause you'll never have a chance. There's a rope waitin' for each o' you. That's the proper way out for such murderin' scum. A bullet's too decent."

"Riley," Whalen said, "I sure take off my sombrero to you. We thought it was all a joke about you chasin' us so long. And you've been a fool to do it. What's it goin' to get you, huh?"

"A lot of satisfaction."

"Yeah? You can't buy anything with satisfaction, Riley. It won't get you wine or high livin', or even grub. You'd be a damned fool to take us in. Everybody'd give you a cheer—and forget it the next minute."

"Well—?" Riley asked.

"We know where there's a cache with plenty dinero in it. Take us there, take what you want, then turn us loose. Clothes there, too, and some grub, so we'll get along."

"How much dinero?" Riley asked.

"Maybe ten thousand, maybe a little less. Take it all. We can get more. Or, if you've got real sense, throw in with us. We'll forget the past and be pals with you."

"You're offerin' to bribe me, huh?" Riley asked.

"We're offerin' you a lot of money just to let us go."

"You're forgettin' one thing—I'm a Ranger."

"They laughed you out of the force," Whalen said. "Here's your chance to get square with 'em."

"I'm still on the force—special detail. Didn't

know that, did you? Never dismissed. Just out
on a little special hunt of my own. Got my
badge fastened on the inside of my boot-top."

"So it's no use?" Bancord asked.

"No use! I'm takin' you in!"

"And a hell of a lot of good it'll do you!"
Whalen cried. "We've got plenty of money for
lawyers. We'll get out on bail and fade away.
Then, Mr. Ranger Riley, we'll take the trail
after you. And when we get you, we'll take you
below the Line, where we've got some Yaqui
friends. They're worse than the Apaches ever
dared be. You'll be prayin' for 'em to kill you.
But I've seen 'em keep a man alive a month,
torturin' him every day. You're a strong man,
Riley—you'd probably last longer."

"I'm takin' you in!" Riley said. "Let's be
gettin' on."

They went on, with two cursing prisoners in
their underwear damning the mounting sun and
its heat, and the stinging flies, and the branches
which flew back into their faces. Over the hills
and down the slope on the opposite side they
traveled. At midday, Riley called a halt beside
a tiny creek.

The horses were watered, and the prisoners
were helped out of their saddles and allowed to

go to the creek to drink, and bathe their hands and faces and sore feet. Then their wrists were lashed behind their backs again.

"Let's travel!" Riley said.

Again, the prisoners were compelled to mount, though Whalen had to be persuaded with a blow on the head. On they went, down the slope, following narrow trails.

"We'll get there before dark," Riley said. "The town'll get a laugh out of you bad hombres."

"We'll get the last laugh, Riley, when the Yaquis are torturin' you," Whalen said.

"You'll never see your Yaqui friends again, Whalen. Nor Bancord, either. And the big deal you were goin' to put over with Kline— I reckon it won't go through. He'll be wonderin' what's become of you, and he'll find your clothes."

"Yeah, and send men on the trail," Bancord added. "And when they catch up with us, I only hope they don't kill you, Riley. 'Cause I want you saved. I want to see you die by inches."

Don Esteban Marcos Pulido turned in his saddle.

"Señor Dan," said he, "I grow weary of the

hombre! He does not seem to realize that he is but a joke. High-sounding words from the throat of a fool! I feel like singing."

"Don't!" Riley warned.

"It is safe, my friend. The countyseat is not more than another hour away. We have saved miles and miles by this cut across the hills. From the top of the next hill, you may see the buildings in the distance."

"That's good news," Riley said. "I suppose you used to run around these here hills when you were a boy, huh?"

"*Sí, señor!* It was my privilege then to learn a quick way from the countyseat to the hills." Esteban chuckled. "I left in disgrace, and now I return in triumph, bringing gifts."

They reached the crest, and, in the far distance, could see the buildings of the town. Down into a jumble of rocks they rode, where there was no trail at all, the horses feeling for safe footing.

Don Esteban Marcos Pulido could contain himself no longer. He began humming a song, and then he muttered the words, and then, when there came no rebuke from Dan Riley, he lifted his voice in earnest.

Riley was riding in advance, and Whalen's

horse was fastened to his saddle with a lariat. Esteban was escorting Bully Bancord in like manner. The horses skidded and lurched, and the ropes grew taut at times.

Both Riley and Esteban were compelled to give all their attention to their mounts to prevent disaster. Esteban's song ceased for the moment.

"There is a good trail when we get to the bottom of the hill," Esteban said. "We follow it to a road, and then go on to the countyseat without further trouble. Señor Dan, I am famished."

"We'll eat plenty," Riley promised.

Whalen tried again. "Better make a deal with us, Riley, before it's too late. You could be fixed for life. More dinero than you could save out of a Ranger's salary in five hundred years."

"And plenty more after that, if you want to throw in with us," Bancord added.

"We can get you in on this big deal we're workin' on now," Whalen said.

"You're wastin' breath, gents," Riley told them. "I can't be bribed. I started out to do a thing, and I'm damned well goin' to do it."

They came presently to the bottom of the hill, let the horses rest for a short time, and then started on at an easy lope. It was a grotesque cavalcade, with the two men on the led horses dressed only in their underwear.

The trail wound through a grove of trees and into some rough ground, where there was a jumble of rocks and crags, a tangle of trees and shrubs and vines.

"Only a short distance more, Señor Dan," Esteban said. "Soon we come to the regular road, where we can make better speed. And then—"

Ahead of them, a gun cracked. The whining bullet flew past Dan Riley's head, struck a rock, went shrieking up the hill to bury itself in the dirt.

CHAPTER XX

AT THE COUNTYSEAT

BACK at the ranch, Kline had connected the escape of Riley and Esteban in his mind with the strange disappearance of Bully Bancord and Hank Whalen.

Going to the adobe hut at daylight to hold a conference with the rogues, Kline had found them missing, but their clothes still there. A quick investigation disclosed four missing horses, including Riley's and that Esteban had ridden out from town.

So Kline called his men to him, and sent them away in pairs. They were to cut off the men and their prisoners, and bring them back, alive if possible. Some took to the hills, looking for a trail. Some hurried toward Mesaville, and others went toward the countyseat. Kline had thought that Riley might make an attempt to deliver his prisoners to the sheriff.

Thus it happened that two of Kline's men heard Esteban's song of triumph, and they went

into ambush and waited for the strange cavalcade to come along.

That shot had been fired at Riley deliberately,
but the marksman had missed. And the next instant Riley and Esteban had their six-guns out,
and were trying to get under cover with their
prisoners.

"Put 'em up, Riley! We'll shoot to kill!"

One of Kline's men howled that at him, but it
had no effect. Dan Riley was not the man to
put up his hands at the order of somebody he
could not even see. He managed to get his horse
behind some rocks, and pull the led horse after
him, and Esteban did the same.

Riley vaulted out of his saddle and tied his
mount to the nearest tree. Esteban sensed his
plan, and did likewise. The prisoners, fastened
in their saddles, and with their hands tied behind
their backs, could not untie the horses and
escape.

But they were not gagged now, and they could
yell. Whalen shouted a warning at his unknown
benefactors. Bancord bellowed advice. Riley
and Esteban went into the brush, six-guns ready,
to meet the enemy.

"Watch out for 'em, boys!" Whalen cried.
"They're sneakin' through the brush."

Kline's men were mounted. One of the horses betrayed their position by a whinny. Riley and Esteban moved in that direction. There was a crashing in the brush, a burst of gunfire, a chorus of wild shouts.

Dan Riley heard Don Esteban Marcos Pulido give a warwhoop that was a great distance from being a song. He caught sight of a man with blazing gun in hand, and recognized him as one he had seen at the ranch. Riley lurched forward, ready to fire.

His boot caught in a trailing vine, and he sprawled forward. He felt a blow high in his shoulder, and knew he had been hit. But he went on, crashing through the brush. Ahead of him, one of Kline's men was fighting to get his horse out of the open. The other had dismounted and taken to cover.

Don Esteban gave another warwhoop and charged through the brush. Riley went after him as rapidly as possible. He got out into a tiny clearing, just in time to see the mounted man topple from his horse. From the brush at Riley's right came another shot. He whirled, threw up his gun, and fired. Headlong, his assailant plunged into the grass.

"Where are you, Señor Dan?" Esteban was shouting.

"Here!" Riley sat down quickly, for he experienced a moment of nausea and weakness.

Esteban came rushing through the brush and up to him.

"I got one of the hombres," he reported.

"Other one—over there. Better look at him —may be only hurt."

"Are you hit, Señor?"

"Yeah! Look at that man first. He may be able to shoot."

Esteban hurried away. Riley closed his eyes a moment, for a thousand red-hot needles seemed to be piercing his shoulder and arm. The fit of weakness passed, and he began to take stock. The wound was nothing serious, he decided, and there would not even be a dangerous loss of blood. He'd have Esteban bandage it.

Esteban came from the brush, carrying the wounded man across his back. He dumped him on the ground near Riley.

"The scoundrel is only wounded in the hip, señor," he reported. "I kicked his gun into the weeds. Now, I shall get the other."

Dan Riley was on his feet when Esteban got the other. He had been shot in the side, low down, the worst wound of the lot. Esteban dumped him on the ground, then went to get the two horses.

They got the wounded men on their horses and lashed them there. Back through the brush they went, to where their prisonere were waiting.

"A longer parade, Señor Dan," Esteban said. "We shall tie the horses all together with ropes, and go down the trail and into town in style. For years, señor, people shall talk of this day."

"Let's get goin'," Riley said.

"Can nothing be done about your own wound, my friend?"

"It'll be all right till we get to town."

"If only I could have suffered it for you!" said Don Esteban Marcos Pulido. And he meant it! . . .

They entered the countyseat an hour before sunset, in the cool of the evening when everybody was out taking the air, causing a sensation. People followed them from the edge of the town to the jail, the crowd continually growing larger.

Esteban, looking straight ahead, was singing, though in a subdued voice. Beside him, Riley rode, hunched forward in the saddle, sick and weak. Behind them came the two prisoners in their underwear, and behind the prisoners, two horses carrying the wounded men lashed in their saddles.

The sheriff and some deputies met them at the door of the jail and got them inside. There was a call for a doctor. Things became orderly and official.

Don Esteban hovered around Riley until the doctor had done his work and assured him there was nothing to fear. Nor would any of the others dodge jail by dying, the physician promised them.

Then Dan Riley, already recuperating swiftly, held a conference with the sheriff, and told him all he had learned, all that had happened in which he had been concerned.

"Good work, boy!" the sheriff praised. "We've wanted these two hombres for a long time. Akers dead, too, eh? That leaves only one."

"Dude Lachmer. Leave him to me, sheriff, please. Let me finish out the deal."

"But you say he'll be due in a few days—and you're a wounded man."

"Only a shot in the shoulder, and my left shoulder at that. I'll be startin' back in the mornin'. I'm worried about Mr. Granton and his daughter as long as Kline's there."

"Then stop worryin'," the sheriff said. "I'm leavin' in an hour with a posse. We'll manage to get there before daylight. I'll 'tend to Mr. Kline."

"That'll be fine!" Riley said.

"Want to send any message to Miss Granton?"

"Me?" Riley asked. "Why, no! I—I'll tell her all about it when I see her. Maybe she won't even be interested."

"She's a damned funny girl, then," the sheriff said. "You bust up a game to steal all the stock on the ranch and put a few bad men out of the way, for her father. If she ain't interested after that, I don't know girls. Maybe you're the one as ain't interested."

"That's it!" Riley said. "I hate women. After what happened to me—"

"Uh-huh!" said the sheriff. "We're all like that, till the right one comes along. You're goin' to bed now, here in my quarters. And you'd better stay there a few days, too. You've sure made good, Riley!"

"I ain't done, though. You keep your hands off Dude Lachmer, sheriff, and leave him to me.

Give me first chance. If I don't handle him, then you can come in."

"Have it your own way, Riley. You want anything else now? I've got to see about gettin' the posse together."

"Just send in Esteban, will you?"

Esteban was waiting, and hurried into the room.

"It was a triumph, Señor Dan!" he cried. "I regret that I have not always led a life of activity. I have been too indolent! Hereafter, I shall follow in your footsteps."

"You hush your damned nonsense, Esteban, and do somethin' for me."

"Anything, señor!"

"Fetch me my hat—and a hot runnin' iron."

Esteban grinned, and hurried from the room.

Riley sat on the edge of the bed and waited. It took some time, but presently Esteban returned, the hat in one hand and the hot iron in the other, and two deputies behind him half convinced that he intended to torture the wounded man.

Dan Riley took the hat and iron, and did the work he so long had wanted to do. From the leather hat band he burned two names—Bancord and Whalen.

"Only one left now," he said, weakly.

"You must have rest!" Don Esteban declared. "Stretch out, and allow me to cover you with the blanket. That is it, señor."

"We start back at daybreak, Esteban."

"As you please, Señor Dan. Turn your head away from the light, and close your eyes. Sleep is what you need."

Don Esteban seemed to forget that he might need some sleep himself, though he was not wounded and had lost no blood. He sat very close to the bed, and bent over slightly. He began humming, and then singing softly, as a mother might have done. And there were tears in the eyes of Don Esteban Marcos Pulido as he watched over the only man who had ever given him real friendship.

CHAPTER XXI

CARMELITA PAYS A VISIT

IT was almost the middle of the morning be-fore they started out, and then against the advice of the doctor. But Dan Riley would not listen to remaining in the countyseat any longer. His job was not done.

His shoulder pained at times, but he did not mind that so much. Don Esteban's merry chat-ter offset the pain, as they rode up into the hills and Esteban sought and found old trails he knew, each one of which meant a short-cut to the Gran-ton ranch.

"We shall be there long before sunset, my friend," he said. "And then we shall see the light in a lady's eyes."

"You're filled with damned foolishness," Riley complained.

"I never did like the golden-haired ones my-self. Give me the snap and fire of one like that Carmelita Lopez, for instance."

"Yeah, she's a snappy girl," Riley said.

"And which would you say, señor, would be

the best for a man were he to marry her?" Esteban eyed him as one who seeks information.

"Neither!" Riley replied, promptly. "Let's get along! We're pokin'!"

"And why are you so eager, señor?"

"I want to get to the ranch and see what's happened, damn it! Dude Lachmer is liable to show up at any time. He'll learn from Drake that Akers is dead, and guess what's happened to Bancord and Whalen. It'll be all over the countryside after the sheriff gets there. Lachmer might take a notion to disappear, pronto. And I don't want to spend another six months or a year chasin' around lookin' for him."

"I see, señor! You wish to settle down."

"How's that?"

"You take me from a peaceful existence, and make a man of action of me. You get me to loving this wild life where a man fights continually. And then you decide to settle down, and leave me without a partner."

"Who the hell said anything about settling down?" Riley wanted to know.

"I merely suggested it," said Don Esteban.

"Don't be suggestin' it. How the blazes can I settle down?"

"Take the job at the Granton ranch. That

will mean that I have to wash pots and pans to
be near you—but in life we must take the bad
things with the good."

"We'll see about that—after I've 'tended to
Dude Lachmer. That's the next job on my list,"
Riley said. "He's the youngest of the bunch,
and the worst. Bad with a gun. Ain't got any
heart at all."

"May I offer my assistance, señor?"

"You keep out of it. You'll be gettin' hurt
yet. Want to get all shot up and have a doctor
paw over you?"

Esteban sighed. "You are greedy, indeed,"
he said. "You would retain all the fun for yourself, and rob others of a share."

It was the middle of the afternoon when they
went over the crest of the range and started
down the slope on the other side. Here the trail
was better, the going faster. Riley's shoulder
was burning, and he knew that it should receive
care. He would be glad to get to the ranch,
where somebody could dress the wound.

Esteban led the way across rough ground until
they came to a trail which ran toward the ranch.
Side by side, they loped along, their neckcloths
up now as protection against the dust. Riley
found that his eyes blurred at times. He grew

dizzy, reeled in the saddle. It was the sun, he kept telling himself—only the sun. He'd be all right when he got to the ranch and could get into some shade.

Over another hill they rode, and in the distance could see the buildings of the ranch.

"Soon now, señor, we shall be there," Don Esteban said, dropping his neckcloth and wiping the perspiration from his face. "You will be a hero. Remember, in the day of your glory, that I am your friend."

Riley made no reply. Esteban turned quickly to look at him—and was just in time to jerk his horse over and keep Riley from toppling from the saddle. . . .

So it happened that Dan Riley returned to consciousness from a realm of grotesque nightmares to find himself in a room he never had seen before. He opened his eyes to contemplate a ceiling with cream-colored wallpaper upon it. He turned his head, and a groan escaped him.

"Oh!" He knew it was a woman gave the exclamation. An instant later he saw her, for she stepped around the bed upon which Riley was stretched.

Betty Granton bent over him, smiled at him, tucked the quilt in a little.

"Don't you remember?" she asked. "You almost fell out of the saddle, and Esteban brought you in. He fired his revolver until some of the men heard and went to help. That was yesterday."

"Yesterday?" Riley did not believe.

"Your wound was worse than you thought, and you must have lost a lot of blood. You'll be all right in a few days. Now, you'd better have something to eat. I'll get it."

"Where am I?" Riley asked.

"In the ranch house, of course. We can't thank you enough, Dan, for what you've done. Dad was in an awful fix. He'd have been blamed for everything."

"Then they didn't get away with anything?"

"The sheriff and his men attended to that. They're here yet, and they're going to stay for a week or so. They're checking up the stock on the range, and watching the trails. Some of the gang have been arrested. They'll get the others when they come over from Mexico to drive back the stock."

"That's fine!" Riley said.

"Kline confessed to the whole thing, and they've sent him away. Now I'll get you something to eat."

"It's a lot of bother," Riley said. "Why not let me go to the bunk house? I don't have to be petted."

"I'm not petting you—don't think it," she said.

"Could I see Esteban?"

"Certainly. He's waiting to see you. He's been worried. Said if he could come in and sing to you, you'd become conscious."

"Yeah? I prob'ly would—long enough to bust him one," Riley said.

She hurried from the room, and, a moment later, Esteban came in. He grinned when he saw Riley looking at him.

"Some men have all the good fortune," Esteban observed. "Did I suffer wound, undoubtedly they would toss me in a corner of the cantina and tell me to get over it. But they tuck you in a bed with white sheets, and give you a pretty girl for a nurse—"

"That'll be enough!" Riley interrupted. "You come closer, and make talk. You heard anything about that Dude Lachmer?"

"I have heard nothing, señor. If he is in the

neighborhood, he has not advertised his presence."

"He prob'ly wouldn't advertise it except with
a six-gun."

"You are not to worry about Lachmer, Señor
Dan. He will have to wait for the pleasure of
being shot by you. The doctor says you must remain in bed for at least a week longer."

"There ain't any doctor alive who can keep me
here a week. I ain't hurt bad."

"If you are not careful, there may be an infec-
tion and a fever. Were I in your place, señor,
I should take a month to get well."

"Yeah, you prob'ly would," Riley told him.
"You listen to me, Esteban. Keep your ears
open. I want to know the minute that Dude
Lachmer comes in this part of the country. I
don't want him to ride on when he learns what's
happened."

"I quite understand, señor. There is a way of
detaining him, perhaps. I can circulate the report in Mesaville that you have said Lachmer is
afraid to meet you. That would hold him here,
would it not?"

"You do that," Riley instructed. "That's just
the thing. Say that I dare him to hang around
Mesaville until I'm well enough to get to town.

Let him know that the sheriff will keep hands off till I have my chance."

Betty Granton came in with a tray, and motioned for Esteban to leave. He bowed himself out backward, and a moment later they heard him singing softly as he descended the stairs.

Riley ate what she had brought.

"It ain't very fillin'," he complained.

"It's food for sick folks. I suppose you want a rare steak about an inch thick."

"I could use one," he said, grinning.

"Not to-day. Now, Dan, there's something else. There's somebody here to see you—drove out from town and got here an hour ago. She wouldn't go away—"

"She?" He looked at her in surprise.

"Carmelita Lopez, the cantina girl. She seems to think a lot of you."

"Yeah? She's the one doped my wine and got me disgraced. But she's been doin' her best to square that. Maybe she's got some news I ought to know."

"Possibly," Betty Granton said. "Do you want to see her?"

"Sure, if it'll be all right. I don't mind tellin' you that she's been gatherin' information for me.

Somethin' she told me gave me the first hint about that plot."

"I'll go and get her, Dan, and send her right in."

CHAPTER XXII

THE CHALLENGE

CARMELITA'S face was white when she entered the bedroom. She had heard that Dan Riley had been terribly wounded. And she was afraid of this big house, and people like Betty Granton, and possibly just a little jealous of the latter, too. But she brightened when Riley smiled at her.

"Howdy, Carmelita!" he greeted. "What you think of this, huh? Got me in bed like some little old woman with heart trouble. On account of one little bullet."

"Señor Dan, they told me you might die!"

"Shucks! Me die? Not for years and years yet. Couldn't die here anyhow, with all the care I'm gettin'. When I get up, reckon I'll be a softie."

"I'll leave you alone," Betty said. There seemed to be a trace of jealousy in her manner, too, as she left the room.

Dan Riley almost laughed at the thought.

He, who hated all women, to have two jealous of him!

"What brought you 'way out here, Carmelita?" Riley asked.

"I felt that I had to come and see you, Señor Dan. I heard so many stories, and no two alike. I was afraid—"

"I ain't goin' to die, if that's what you're afraid of. Almost fell off my horse, 'count the heat, and Esteban brought me in. Then the fool doctor said I had to stay in bed. I'm strong enough to hear any news you've brought me."

"It is about Dude Lachmer, señor. He is coming up from Mexico, and probably will get to Mesaville to-morrow."

"You reckon he knows what's happened around here?"

"*Sí, señor!* He has learned that you are here, and that Sam Akers is dead. He may not know about the two others. But he has said, Señor Dan, that he intends to—" She stopped.

"Intends to get me, huh? That's all right. I'm intendin' to get him, too. We'll see who's right."

"You must not think of meeting with him, señor, until you are well. They say he is swift and clever with a gun."

"He's all o' that. Got nerve, too. Ain't afraid of anything. Anything else, Carmelita?"

"Only that I hope, señor, you'll be safe."

"How's that?"

"Being wounded and in bed, señor, you are helpless. You, who hate women so! If the girl with the yellow hair—"

"Harpin' on that again, are you? Stop it!"

"Do you hate women, señor, only because of what I did, because I caused you to be laughed at and disgraced?"

"I never hated 'em before," he said.

"You should not blame them all, señor, for my fault. I am only a silly girl. The Señorita Granton—she probably never would do such a thing."

"If you came here to talk to me about women, you can danged well get home again, pronto," he said.

"I came to tell you about Dude Lachmer, and ask if there is anything I can do."

"Do anything to keep him in Mesaville till I can get there. I told Esteban the same. I don't want that hombre to get away from me again. With his pals gone, he might never come back to this part of the country. And I've got to have my record clean. Understand?"

"I understand, señor," she said. "Dude Lachmer shall stay in Mesaville until you are able to meet him."

Then Betty Granton came back into the room, and Carmelita got up and smiled at Riley again, and went away. And Don Esteban Marcos Pulido returned, to sit beside the bed and watch while Riley slept, and so give Betty Granton a chance to get some rest. Esteban knew she had been at the bedside from the moment Riley had been brought there—but Riley did not know that. . . .

Riley was able to dress partially and get downstairs the following day, there to sit on the wide veranda and watch the men working around the barns and corrals, and down by the bunk house.

"She is a great outfit, this Granton ranch," Esteban told him. "A splendid outfit, señor. It will be a pleasure to wash pots and pans."

"So you're goin' to take that job?" Riley asked.

"You are my friend, and I would be near you."

"Who told you I'm goin' to be here?"

"I just know it, señor."

"Don't forget that I've got a little engagement in Mesaville when I'm able to get there. After

that, I might not be able to hold down a job any
place."

Esteban looked at him soberly. "I am not
afraid, Señor Dan," he said. "It is not in the
cards that I should find a friend and lose him so
soon."

"You're one good hombre, Esteban! Help
me upstairs again, now. I don't want to overdo
it the first day. I've got to get on my feet."

The following day he remained in bed, but
the day after that he was allowed to dress and
go downstairs again, and this time he went with
Esteban down to the corral and had a visit with
his horse.

No news had come from Mesaville regarding
Dude Lachmer. They did not know whether he
had arrived. But that evening a man returned
from town with the mail, and he reported that
he had a note for Riley, which was given him.
Carmelita had written it, and Riley imagined
the labor it had cost her. Only a few words, but
they said that Dude Lachmer had been in Mesaville two days, and was waiting.

"I've got to get on my feet, Esteban," Riley
said. "That hombre will be thinkin' I'm afraid
to come into town."

"Perhaps, señor, I could go in and settle the affair for you," Esteban said.

"Would that give me the chance to burn his name off my hat band? I'll do the settlin'. There's one hombre I wish I could take in alive. I'd admire to watch him stretch rope. Killed two men when he didn't have to do it—just 'cause he loves killin'."

"Such a man should die," Esteban said.

"I'm sure hopin' that I'll feel stronger to-morrow. Feel a lot better to-day. How much longer is the sheriff and his gang goin' to hang around here?"

"For several days yet, señor. It is expected that certain men will come across the Line to pick up stock, and the sheriff wishes to catch them at it."

"There's one fight I'll miss, I suppose."

"Must you be in all of them, señor? Would it not be wise to allow the sheriff to earn his wages?" Esteban asked.

Riley grinned. "One good hombre!" he voiced again.

He felt stronger the following day, and walked down to the big bunk houses and inspected them, and talked to some of the punchers. He also ate the noon meal at the family table, and listened to Granton explaining his ideas for making the ranch bigger and better yet.

Then he went out to sit on the veranda again. Betty went for a ride with one of the men, waving at him from the lane. Esteban journeyed down to the calf pasture to look at some of the fancy stock. Granton himself had gone to the office, for he was compelled to do Kline's work until a new superintendent could be appointed.

So Dan Riley was alone on the veranda when a rider came loping down the lane toward the big house. He shaded his eyes with his hands and tried to make identification, but could not. The rider did not turn down toward the corrals, but came on toward the veranda steps.

Riley recognized him, then, as a man he had seen in Mesaville. He got out of the saddle and strode forward, and called from the bottom of the steps.

"Ain't you Dan Riley?"

"Yeah!"

"I've got a letter for you, then. A hombre in Mesaville paid me to leave it here, me bein' on my way past."

He ascended the steps, came along the veranda railing, and handed Riley the letter.

"Who's it from?" Riley asked.

"I didn't read it, mister. I don't read other folks' letters."

"I didn't say you did, damn it. I mean, who gave it to you?"

"I don't know his name—hombre who hangs around the cantina a lot. Don't think he wrote it. Think somebody gave it to him to give me."

"Sit down while I read it."

"Ain't got time. I'm bound for the Cross Bar ranch, and want to get there before dark."

He went down the steps, mounted, and galloped up the lane. Riley watched until he disappeared in a dust cloud out on the trail, then ripped the envelope open.

It was as he had expected—the note was from Dude Lachmer. Riley's face burned as he read it:

> *How much longer are you going to bluff about being hurt, so you won't have to meet up with me?*
>
> LACHMER.

Esteban was walking up from the corral now, and Riley called to him, and handed him the note to read.

"Do not let it worry you, my friend," Esteban

said. "It is but a trick of this Señor Lachmer to get you to fight when he will have the advantage."

"He says I'm bluffin' about bein' hurt."

"We know that is not the truth, señor."

"Yeah, but a lot of other folks don't know it. Lachmer will be tellin' that yarn around, and I couldn't stand people thinkin' I was afraid to meet up with him. It's time for a showdown, Esteban. I'll burn that last name off my hat band, or—"

"There can be no 'or,' señor," Esteban interrupted. "Certainly, you must burn off the last name. It is a thing to be expected."

"We're goin' to Mesaville this evenin'."

"Señor!" Esteban gasped.

"Right after it gets dark. Don't you tell anybody, 'cause they might want to stop me. You can go along."

"But certainly, Señor Dan! I would not allow you to go alone."

"Right after it's dark, you get the horses ready. Tell the corral guard anything you can think of. Take the horses down the lane to the well."

"I understand, señor."

"I'm usin' that room on the lower floor of the

house now. I can slip through the window, and they won't miss me. You get the horses ready, and wait."

"Don't you think, señor, that it would be better to wait yet one more day?" Esteban begged. "You do not realize how weak you are."

"You think, after that note, I'd wait another day? How many men do you s'pose he showed that note to before he sent it out here? Don't you worry about me bein' weak. The ride in the cool night air will brace me up. And one shot will be enough. You get them horses ready!"

CHAPTER XXIII

RILEY ANSWERS THE NOTE

A LITTLE after dark, Dan Riley, who had been sitting in the ranch house parlor with the others, excused himself and went to his room. He was tired, he said, and wanted a good rest, and perhaps the following day he would be stronger.

He sat beside the window for a time, listening to the drone of the voices in the outer room. Then he locked the door and turned out the light, as though he had retired.

He dressed slowly, trying not to exert himself too much, taking plenty of time about it. Esteban might be some time getting the horses ready, he knew. But finally he buckled on his gun-belt, swung the holster back, and put on his hat.

Going across to a window, he unlatched it and raised it a bit at a time, careful not to make any noise. The drone of voices out in the parlor continued. Riley got through the window, and for a moment braced himself against the side of the house.

He felt better, and started going through the shadows to the front. The big trees along the lane kept the moonlight from exposing him. He made for the well, where he had told Esteban to wait.

But Riley did not have to wait long, for Esteban soon came through the shadows toward him, riding a ranch horse and leading Riley's own mount. He helped Riley up into the saddle, and they rode slowly down the lane and away from the house, unheard.

When they turned into the dusty road, they went at a fair rate of speed through the moonlight, and toward the first hill. There they stopped for a breathing spell. Esteban tendered a canteen, and Riley drank.

"How do you feel, señor?" Esteban asked.

"I'm feelin' better every minute," Riley declared. "I'll be strong enough by the time we get to town. What I needed was exercise and fresh air."

"It would be better to proceed slowly, señor."

"We ain't goin' to rush it," Riley told him. "But we ain't goin' to lag much, either. I've got it figured out, Esteban. We'll get to town about the time the crowd's thickest at the cantina. Afraid to come in and meet him, am I? I'll meet him where everybody can see."

They rode on toward the distant pass, letting the horses have an easy pace. Riley eased his body in the saddle as much as possible. At times, he pulled the horse down to a walk.

In the pass, the cold night wind rushed through, and Riley felt that it braced him. He seemed to be gathering strength. On the other side of the pass, where the trail was deep with dust, they put up their neckcloths, and ceased conversation.

Riley began thinking of his chase and its culmination. Akers dead. Bancord and Whalen in jail and bound for the gallows. Dude Lachmer, the worst of the lot considered from any angle, in Mesaville waiting for a duel.

Only Lachmer stood between him and vindication. If he disposed of Lachmer, he could go back and face his old captain again. Then he would turn in his badge, and consider his work at an end, and return to the Granton ranch and settle down to a prosaic job at so much a month and found.

He was not underestimating either Lachmer or the situation. Lachmer was good with a gun, swift and accurate. He was not easily caught off guard. He was not afraid. Under normal conditions, he would have been a fair match, Riley knew. And these were not normal conditions.

For, despite what he had boasted to Esteban, Riley knew that he was half sick, and weak. His eyes blurred at times. He had spells of dizziness. He would have to nerve himself for the ordeal, have it over with quickly.

After a time they topped a hill from the crest of which they could see twinkling lights in the distance—Mesaville. They stopped for a moment, drank water, made and lighted cigarettes, rested.

"How do you feel, señor?" Esteban asked.

"I'm feelin' better every minute, sure enough," Riley said.

"If you could only wait for another day—"

"No more waitin'," Riley interrupted. "I won't have that skunk tellin' folks that I'm afraid, and delayin' on purpose. And it's got to be ended, so why not to-night?"

"As you will, señor. It would be a pleasure for me to remove this man for you."

"Prob'ly he'll be in the cantina," Riley said. "We'll try to spot where he is before we go in. All I want is a fair chance. Don't want to take any advantage, and don't want to give any. Let's ride!"

They continued along the trail, watching the twinkling lights of the distant town blinking at them through the clear air. On a gust of wind came the din of the cantina—the piano being hammered, somebody singing, loud voices, laughter.

Dan Riley caught himself wondering whether this was the last time he ever would hear the sounds. He had a vision of the burial of Bill Morgan on the hill back of the town, and shuddered. But he nerved himself again at the next instant, told himself that he would be the victor if there was a clash.

They came to the corner of the plaza and stopped their horses in the shadow of the blacksmith shop. Esteban tendered the canteen again, and Riley drank deeply.

"Plenty o' time," Riley said. "I think I'll have another smoke, Esteban."

"Sí, señor!" Esteban said. "It is a tonic for the nerves."

Riley rolled a cigarette. His hands were not shaking at all now. The weakness seemed to have left him, and new strength to flow into his body, as though purposely for the ordeal he faced. He snapped a match and ignited the smoke, and puffed slowly.

"Your hand is steady, señor?" Esteban asked.

"Never better, old-timer!"

"Is there anything I may do to be of service?"

"Not a thing, unless you just keep your eyes open and see that it's a square deal. I don't mind bracin' myself up to fight one man, but I ain't in any condition to fight more."

"I shall watch carefully," Esteban said.

"Let's go, then. We'll tie up our horses at the cantina. I don't reckon he'd jump me foul. Dude Lachmer 'd want to show off. He'll want to fight under the bright lights, with a lot of folks watchin' him." . . .

Back at the Granton ranch, Granton thought that he would look in upon Riley before he went to bed, and see if he was asleep. He found the door locked, which was unusual.

Granton called a man to him, sent him outside and around to the window, and he got through and unlocked the door.

"He ain't here! Bed ain't been slept in!"

Granton entered with a lamp, holding it high and throwing the light all around the room.

"And the window was open all the way up," the cowpuncher added.

Betty heard them, and came hurrying from her own room, fearing that Riley had grown worse. It was Betty who found the note.

"Dad!" she cried. "Read this! That's where he's gone. Into town, to fight that man! Please! See if the horses are gone. See if Esteban is gone, too. Oh, Dad! He—he'll be killed!"

"And would you care, honey?" her father asked.

She lifted her face, and he read her eyes. A moment later, John Granton was bellowing orders.

The big ranch bell clanged, and men tumbled out of their bunks and into their clothes. Other men came running to make reports.

Riley's horse was gone, and another also. Esteban could not be found. One of the men said he had heard somebody riding down the lane.

"Dad!" Betty begged.

The punchers were gathered around the veranda steps, and the sheriff and some of his deputies came hurrying from the bunk house. Granton looked down at them all.

"Riley got an insulting letter from that outlaw, Dude Lachmer, to-day," Granton said. "He said Riley was faking about being sick, was afraid to come in and fight him. And Riley's gone in to fight. Saddle up, some of you. Get my horse ready. We'll ride to Mesaville, and see that he gets a square deal!"

"Saddle my black!" Betty cried to one of the men. She rushed back into the house to dress in riding clothes.

"I think I'll take a hand in this here game myself," the sheriff said. "I ain't had a wild night ride for quite a spell. And, if anything happens to Dan Riley—then I want a few words with Dude Lachmer!"

CHAPTER XXIV

A GENUINE FRIEND

OUT of the lane and into the dusty road the riders of the Granton outfit swept through the moonlight, headed by John Granton and his daughter, the sheriff and some of his deputies riding with them.

They began to string out along the road as they gathered speed for the long run. Clouds of dust lifted behind them, to be picked up by the night wind and shifted to settle anew on rocks and grass and brush.

They rode with their neckcloths up and hats pulled down against the tear of the wind. Over the first hill they swept, and down the slope, went around the big curve, and started toward the pass.

Riley and Esteban had started a long time before them, but had ridden slowly. And these did not spare horseflesh in their mad chase. At the head of the flying cavalcade, Betty Granton urged her big black to better speed, and her father kept pace with her. Gradually, they drew away from the others.

Into the little pass they went, after a time, to slow down because of the treacherous footing. Here, they bunched together again. And when they emerged they were off once more on a wild chase, with Betty and her father leading the way.

Came the time when they could see the lights of the town in the distance. The horses were winded now, and the going was slower. Betty and her father drew ahead of the others again, and, when they came to the last steep hill, had a chance to talk as their mounts walked.

"Maybe you'd better hang back, Betty," Granton said. "It might not be a nice sight for a girl."

"But I want to know, Dad," she told him.

"I reckon we'll find out soon enough, if anything's happened."

"If it hasn't, why doesn't the sheriff arrest that Lachmer man? Then Dan wouldn't have to fight him."

"You don't understand man's way of reasoning, honey. That wouldn't do at all. Riley never would be satisfied all his life. He'd know that there was a job he'd left undone, that somebody else had done for him. He started out to get those four men, and he's got three of them. He wants to get the last."

"But he's been wounded—he's sick. He was so weak yesterday that he staggered when he went out on the porch."

"I reckon that note upset him," Granton said. "It was a kind of challenge to his manhood, and he felt he had to answer it. Maybe you haven't anything to worry about. But I can't understand you. You've never paid much attention to men. And Dan Riley comes along, and without hardly knowing him—"

"I can't explain it myself, Dad," she interrupted. "Oh, let's hurry!"

"Let the men catch up with us. We may need them. Some of the crooks connected with that crowd might be in town, and they'll resent the fact that their scheme's busted. I'm not a bit worried with the boys at my back, and the sheriff's men, too. If they're there, we'll clean them out!"

The lagging riders were coming up to them. They moved forward again in a body, and Granton purposely kept the pace reduced so there would be no straggling. Back in the crowd, the sheriff was bellowing orders to his men.

As they neared the plaza, some rode off to

right and left. They were surrounding the place, quietly, efficiently, like a troop of cavalry. Granton's men were well trained, and a few words sufficed for orders.

"Let's hurry, Dad," Betty Granton begged.

"I'm waiting for the sheriff. Here he comes."

The sheriff rode up to them. "The men are scattered, so we can go ahead, Granton," he said. "Big crowd at the cantina. Bunch of smugglers passin' through, I reckon. We might pick up somethin' good this trip, seein' as how it wasn't prearranged, and hence tipped off."

"Let's hurry!" Betty repeated.

"I reckon Miss Betty'd better stay behind a bit," the sheriff said. "Might get in the way and get hurt, if there's any lead flyin' around. If I hadn't promised Dan Riley, I'd hunt out that Dude Lachmer and take him in myself. But Riley's entitled to his chance."

"What chance has he—a weak, sick man?" Betty cried at him.

"I've seen him shoot," said the sheriff. "Dan Riley sick is a lot better shot than most men well. And then—"

He stopped and glanced ahead. The din in the cantina had died down abruptly. The sheriff

knew the symptoms.   He kicked his horse with
the spurs.

A shot rang out, another—and others.   Then
there was a chorus of wild yells.

The sheriff dashed ahead, shrieking com-
mands to some of the men nearest him.   Granton
pounded along behind, with Betty at his side.
From every direction, Granton ranch punchers
and deputies converged upon the cantina of
Pablo Lopez. . . .

Riley and Esteban had ridden slowly out of
the darkness beside the blacksmith shop and
started across the plaza.

"Señor, I have a thought," Esteban said.   "You
ride over by the stable and remain there in your
saddle for a time.   Rest, and prepare yourself."

"I'm ready right now, Esteban."

"Please allow me to go to the cantina first
alone.   It is not only Dude Lachmer of whom I
am thinking.   But it might be a good thing to
spy out the land.   Others may be ready to play
a hand in the game, señor.   I would not put it
past them.   You have ruined their plans, and
possibly they have sworn to remove you."

"Think they've planned somethin' like that?"

"That note might have been but a decoy, señor.

You do not know Lachmer's handwriting. Or, he may have sent the note—and have men ready to shoot you down."

"It's true that they're an ambushin' gang," Riley admitted. "Go ahead, Esteban, if it'll please you any. Spy out the land. I'll wait over by the stable."

Riley rode away through the shadows, came to the stable wall, and stopped his mount in the darkness there. He saw Don Esteban stop at the end of the crowded hitch rail and find a place to tie up his horse.

Esteban slapped the trail dust from his clothes, removed his riding gauntlets and tucked them into his belt, and rubbed his fingers briskly to get the stiffness out of them. Then he hitched up his chaps and went slowly to the cantina door.

To-night the place was thronged with men off the trail, and with strangers regarding whom Esteban knew nothing and could guess but little. They were three deep at the bar, and all the games were going. The piano was being punished. Some of the cantina girls were dancing.

Esteban stepped inside the door and stood to one side, pretending to be busy with the manufacture of a cigarette. Over the cupped hands which held the flaming match, he glanced around the big room.

Almost immediately he saw Pete Drake, his left arm in a sling because of the wounded shoulder Riley had given him, talking to one of his close friends. Several of Drake's cronies were scattered through the crowd, glancing frequently at the door.

Down by the middle of the bar, there was a sudden gale of laughter, and Esteban glanced that way quickly. He saw a man he supposed was Dude Lachmer—a young, good-looking man dressed in the height of fashion. His clothes were fine, and his boots finer.

But he wanted to be sure this was Dude Lachmer. So he began working through the jostling crowd, trying to avoid attracting attention, and approaching the man who had laughed.

He got quite close to him, tried to get nearer, hoping that somebody would call him by name. The throng parted suddenly, and Dude Lachmer caught sight of Esteban staring at him.

"Hello, Goggleyes!" Lachmer cried. "Who are you lookin' at?"

His right hand shot out and grasped the collar of Esteban's coat. He jerked Esteban to him, breast to breast, and glared down into his eyes. Then he released him a little, and laughed.

"Who are you, Fat Boy?" he asked.

"Señor, I am Don Esteban Marcos—"

"A Don, huh?" Lachmer cried, laughing again. "A fat one!"

"Please to let me go, señor," Esteban said.

"Why were you standin' there and starin' at me? Anything funny about me?" Lachmer demanded. "Feel like laughin'?"

"I did not mean to stare," Esteban said. "I would not be so rude."

"I can tell you who he is, Lachmer," a voice called. Pete Drake thrust his way through the crowd. "He's hooked up with Dan Riley. Rides around with him all the time. Prob'ly in here now spyin' for him."

"So!" Dude Lachmer's eyes grew narrow and seemed to burn. His mouth became a thin, straight line. The expression of the killer came into his face. "Riley's man, huh? That right?"

"I have been working for him, señor," Esteban said.

"What kind of work?" Lachmer snapped.

It is given every man, some time during his life, to have a heroic. Esteban had one now, though he felt that he faced Death at the moment.

"Señor Lachmer, that was a lie," he corrected. "I do not work for Señor Dan Riley. He is my friend, and I am his."

"And you've got the guts to stand there and tell that to me?" Lachmer cried.

Men suddenly scattered away from them, fearful of flying lead. Lachmer whirled Esteban back against the bar and shook him. Esteban's face turned white.

"Sí, señor!" he said. "I am his friend, señor, and proud to be!"

Dude Lachmer whipped out his gun and thrust the muzzle of it against Esteban's breast. Some there turned their faces away quickly. Cantina girls gave cries of pity, and covered their faces with their hands. Men resented it, but did not have the courage to interfere.

"Hombre," Dude Lachmer said, "are you still sayin' that you're proud to be Dan Riley's friend?"

Esteban opened his eyes wide, then closed them. His lips moved silently, and then: "I am proud, señor, to be the friend of Dan Riley!" he said.

Duke Lachmer returned his gun to its holster. He released Don Esteban, and stepped back.

"I wish to Heaven I had a friend like you," he said. "So you call yourself Don, huh? And that's what you are! Everybody should call you Don. . . . Now, if you're Riley's friend, get the hell away from me! Hurry, before I change my mind!"

Esteban walked away through the crowd, his body erect and his eyes shining. But whether they were shining with fear or pride, no man could tell.

CHAPTER XXV

THE MOMENT APPROACHES

DON ESTEBAN stopped in the doorway. Calmly, he made a cigarette and lighted it. The din had broken out behind him again.

Somebody touched him on the shoulder, and he turned slowly to find Pete Drake at his elbow.

"Where's Riley?" Drake asked.

"Somewhere around, señor. I am separated from him for the moment."

"You're liable to be separated from him forever, hombre," Drake said.

Esteban drew himself up. "Are you presuming to threaten me, señor?" he demanded, in a shrill voice.

Instantly, the din was quiet again. That shrill voice had carried. Scores turned to look toward the door. Pete Drake, enraged, did not notice the attention he was attracting.

"I'll threaten you all I like, you worm!" Drake howled. "You tell me where Riley is, and be damned quick about it!"

"Why do you not seek him out yourself, señor?" Esteban asked. "Why not do so openly, instead of sneaking up to the window of his room and trying to murder him in his bed, as you did the other night? How is your sore shoulder, señor? Do you remember what Dan Riley told you? The next time, he said, the bullet would go through your heart."

"Why, you—you—! You dare stand there and talk to me like that?" Drake screeched.

"Why not, señor?" Don Esteban asked. "Can it be that you think I fear you?"

Now there was dead silence in that end of the room. Those who had heard expected a roar of rage to come from the throat of Pete Drake, expected him to whip out his gun and empty its contents into Esteban's breast.

Drake seemed stunned for a moment. His hand was resting against Esteban's arm, and now Esteban reached up and brushed it off. There was dignity in the gesture.

"You—you—" Drake sputtered.

"You annoy me, señor," Esteban said. "Your breath is foul with stale liquor and tobacco, and the medicine on your shoulder nauseates me. There is a horse trough, señor, behind the blacksmith shop. It is my suggestion that you use it."

Somebody in the crowd snickered. Pete Drake saw red. This time, he grasped Esteban and hurled him back against the wall, and followed with his own body so swifty that Esteban had no chance to draw a weapon.

But Drake went no further. His arm was gripped as though by a vise, and he was whirled around forcibly himself, to find the beady eyes of Dude Lachmer boring into his.

"That's enough!" Lachmer said. "You got what was comin' to you, Drake. Hands off this hombre, or you'll answer to me."

"If he's a friend of yours—" Drake said, the suggestion of a sneer in his voice.

"He's a friend of Dan Riley. And I'm goin' to kill Riley as soon as I set eyes on him, or he'll kill me. That's pretty well understood. But our fight is with Dan Riley, and not with his friends unless they take a hand. Understand?"

Drake's face paled beneath that beady glare, and he backed away. Don Esteban went on through the door and out into the night. The crowd resumed its hilarity.

Drake stepped close to Lachmer. "If that hombre's around here, it means that Riley ain't far away," Drake said.

"What of it? When we meet, we'll meet.

Dan Riley ain't the kind to shoot through a window."

"If he gets you, Dude, I'll get him!"

Lachmer laughed. "A fine chance you'd have of gettin' him, if I couldn't! Unless you got him in the back. You've sure messed up things around here, Drake. And now the whole deal's busted."

"Riley busted it."

"Yeah! Riley busted it. Akers comes in here ragin' mad and Riley gets him. No man can gunfight when he's ragin' mad. And Riley goes out to Granton's place and makes fools out of Bancord and Whalen. And now Riley's in Mesaville, about to mix it with me."

"You'll get him, Dude. He's weak and sick yet from his wound."

"I'll make a good try," Lachmer said. "If he gets me—well, it's on the cards."

Lachmer left Drake and made his way through the crowd to the middle of the bar again. Standing there, he could watch the entire room in the big mirror on the back bar. He was a distance from the front and rear doors. It was a position of advantage.

Moreover, he had a man watching each door. He would know the moment Dan Riley came into the cantina. There would be no undue advantage for Riley.

Dude Lachmer was a peculiar individual none could understand. He had killed ruthlessly when the slaying could have been avoided, and then had risked his life in behalf of a man of whom he knew nothing. He was a traitor to his associates at times, yet admired loyalty in others. And he was a fatalist.

Now he beckoned Pablo Lopez to him, and bent over the bar.

"A drink of your finest private stock, Lopez," he ordered.

"Certainly, señor!" Lopez got a bottle from beneath the bar.

Dude Lachmer tossed a gold coin down upon the table. "Keep it, Lopez, but do not mix it with the others just yet."

"Señor?"

"It will be a luck piece, if anything happens to me to-night. The last coin I spent—understand? A blood coin!"

"Señor!" There was horror in Lopez's voice now.

Lachmer laughed. "Why shiver?" he asked. "What is to happen, will happen. It is on the cards. And the little señorita—the delicious

Carmelita—she doesn't like me.   Don't blame her a bit for that, Lopez.   But, if anything happens, buy her something to remember me by, out of the gold piece.   It'll bring her good luck, too."

"Do not talk so, señor," Lopez begged.   "It is terrible to have such things happen in my cantina.   The floor will be drenched with blood."

"Pay some peon to clean it up—out of the gold piece," Lachmer said, laughing again.   "First thing you know, you won't have any of the gold piece left for yourself.   Anyhow, if I pass out to-night, it'll be in the way I want to go.   Bancord and Whalen—they'll swing and kick on the gallows, I reckon.   Nothing like that for Dude Lachmer!"

He tossed off the drink, saluted those around him with the empty glass, and smashed it into fragments against the floor.

"Dan Riley is coming!" somebody called.

CHAPTER XXVI

DON ESTEBAN MARCOS PULIDO, feeling every inch his name, had gone forth into the night and crossed to where Riley was waiting. He related what had occurred.

"He's a queer duck," Riley said. "He'd never surrender and stand trial. The others are wiped out, and maybe he's expectin' the same thing."

"And how do you feel now, señor?" Esteban asked.

"Pretty fair. The little rest did me good."

"I have brought a flask—"

"Afterward," said Riley, "if I am able."

"The cantina is crowded, Señor Dan. Lachmer stands in the middle of the bar."

"Yeah? He needn't be afraid that I'll sneak up on him. I just want everybody else to get out of the way. No sense in hurtin' other folks."

Riley got out of the saddle, and stretched himself while Esteban held the reins. He flexed his muscles, worked his hands. He snapped his six-gun out of its holster a few times, and brought the holster forward a little.

"Let's go, Esteban!" he said.

Side by side they walked across the corner of the plaza, Esteban leading Riley's horse. When they came to the hitch rail, they stopped, and Esteban tied the horse there.

"If anything happens to me, Esteban, the mount is yours," Riley said. "And if you don't treat him right, I'll come back and haunt you."

"Do not speak like that, señor, for the love of the saints—"

"Keep your head up!" Riley advised him. "Who's goin' into this gun duel, you or me?"

"The only true friend I ever had!"

"You haven't lost me yet," Riley said. "If I come out of this all right, you know what kind o' future you've got—cleanin' pots and pans out at the Granton ranch."

They went on toward the open door of the cantina, through which was pouring a medley of music, talk and laughter. Somebody saw them, and gave the alarm: .

"Dan Riley is coming!"

There was an instant hush in the big room. Men moved swiftly, some to get back against the walls, some to leave by the rear door. The middle of the room was cleared.

Dude Lachmer remained standing alone in the middle of the bar, leaning upon it, surveying himself in the mirror. A cigarette drooped from a corner of his mouth. With hands that did not shake at all, he struck a match and ignited it, and puffed as though not concerned with anything in all the world.

Dan Riley stepped through the door, with Esteban close behind him. The latter went slowly aside and joined a group against the wall. Riley looked down the length of the room, scrutinizing the man he had come to get.

Lachmer puffed at the cigarette and continued to survey himself in the mirror. Both his hands were upon the bar, to show that he sought no unfair advantage. Here were two men about to try to kill each other, yet each trusted the other to be fair. Square gamblers for the biggest stakes of all!

Dan Riley backed against the wall, brought forth materials, and made a cigarette of his own. That was a gesture. All things must be equal, even to the chance of getting smoke in the eyes at the crucial moment. Nor did his hand shake when he struck a match and lighted the smoke.

Then, his arms swinging easily at his sides, Dan Riley started down the middle of the room. His eyes never left Lachmer now. He could hear men breathing heavily, heard some cantina girl give a dry sob.

"Lachmer!"

Riley spoke the word in an ordinary tone of voice.

"Howdy, Riley!" Lachmer said. "Been a long time since we saw each other, huh? I understand you've been doin' some runnin' around tryin' to find me."

"Yeah, a little."

"Was you wantin' to see me about anything in particular, Riley?"

"Little matter of murder, Lachmer. You're wanted. Half a dozen charges, if I'm rememberin' right."

"Uh-huh! You still a Ranger?"

"Yeah! On special detached service, though. But everything's official."

"I see," Lachmer said. "Murder, huh? That's right down serious, if they pin it on a man. Never can tell what a jury will do. I've got a bad reputation, too, so they prob'ly wouldn't be very merciful."

"I reckon they wouldn't," Riley admitted.

"Just what are you goin' to do about it, Riley?"

"First thing, I'm askin' you to come peaceable, which is the law."

"I reckon I couldn't think of doin' that."

"I didn't suppose you would," Dan Riley told him. "Had to ask you, though."

"Sure! I understand."

Men in that big room were at the point of screaming. Why didn't they end it? How long were they going to toy with each other, each waiting for the other to make the first move?

"What happens, Riley, when I say I won't surrender?" Dude Lachmer asked.

"Then it's my job to take you, Lachmer, or—"

"Uh-huh! Well?"

"Whenever you're ready, Lachmer, go for your gun!"

Riley's voice changed as he said that. There was a ring in it. He bent forward a bit, and his arms ceased swinging at his sides, and seemed to become rigid.

Dude Lachmer turned slowly from the bar, moving his hands carefully until they were at his sides. Still cautious about taking an unfair advantage.

One of the cantina girls gave a cry: "Oh, I can't stand this! I can't!"

Then the silence again. Neither Lachmer nor Riley had moved. They had scorned to take advantage of the slight shock the girl's scream had caused.

"Whenever you're ready, Lachmer!" Riley repeated.

Like a marble statue, Dude Lachmer stood in the middle of the room a few feet from the bar. The ghost of a smile flashed across his face. And his right hand flashed to his holster.

Dan Riley swerved sharply to one side as he saw the move. Both guns barked, cracked again. Another crack—and a girl's scream!

Something had happened off to one side, but Riley did not look to see. Six-gun still held ready, he started a slow advance. Dude Lachmer had swayed forward slightly, and his gun hand had dropped. And now, with all his strength of will, he was trying to bring it up again. Inch by inch he lifted it.

But strength suddenly left him. His gun dropped from his nerveless fingers and clattered to the floor. Dude Lachmer half turned, collapsed. As he rolled over, the ghost of a smile was on his face again.

"Written . . . on the cards . . ." he said.

Then Dan Riley reeled back against the bar and dropped his own gun, and Esteban gave a cry and was the first to rush across the room toward him. He clutched Riley, held him up.

"Señor Dan! You are hurt?"

Riley turned and looked at him, swayed against him. "So weak," he muttered. "Shoulder—hurts."

Somebody behind the bar shoved a glass of brandy across it, and Esteban put it to Riley's lips. He sipped the liquor, tried to brace himself against the bar, and finally stood erect.

"You could not see, Señor Dan, because you were watching Lachmer," Esteban whispered. "Drake tried to shoot you in the back. And Señorita Carmelita sprang before him."

"What?" Riley cried.

Then he looked across the room. Carmelita was stretched on the floor, her weeping father bending over her, the cantina girls hovering near.

Riley staggered toward them. "What—?" he questioned again.

"And I shot the Señor Drake, straight between the eyes," Esteban added. "It was a very great pleasure, señor!"

Riley sensed what had happened now. He hurried forward as swiftly as his wobbly legs would carry him. They made room for him, and he knelt beside the girl.

Carmelita opened her eyes, saw him, smiled at him a wan little smile.

"I am glad to save you, Señor Dan," she whispered. "I, who once caused you so much trouble. And please to remember, Señor Dan—sometimes a woman, she is good for something."

"You poor kid!" Riley sobbed.

"Do not cry, Señor Dan. I am happy, to do it for you. And—Carmelita tells you this—the girl with the golden hair and blue eyes—she loves you. I see it in her face—that first day." . . .

Then there came a thunder of hooves out in front of the cantina, and men were shouting to one another, and into the big room they rushed, the punchers and the sheriff's men. But they stopped abruptly at the scene they saw.

Dude Lachmer was dead with a smile on his face. Drake was stretched lifeless on the floor. And Carmelita Lopez was clasped in her father's arms, and Dan Riley weeping unashamed over her.

Then Betty Granton rushed in and up to them. And she, too, stopped abruptly at the scene. She watched until Dan Riley got up, and turned, and came toward her.

"Oh, Dan!" she said. "I was so afraid!"

"I—I'm all right, Betty. That poor kid—she saved my life. She atoned, Betty, double over. And she told me somethin', and I want to tell you now, though maybe it don't seem right."

"What did she tell you, Dan?"

"She said you loved me—that she'd seen it in your face the day I stopped your horse."

Betty Granton hung her head a bit. "A woman always knows such things, Dan," she said. . . .

And so Don Esteban Marco Pulido got to sing plenty of love songs after all, and even a lullaby or two a little later on.

THE END